THE LAST SHIP

JAN LOWE SHINEBOURNE

THE LAST SHIP

PEEPAL TREE

First published in Great Britain in 2015
Peepal Tree Press Ltd
17 King's Avenue
Leeds LS6 1QS
England

ISBN13: 9781845232467

Supported using public funding by
ARTS COUNCIL
ENGLAND

For Anne Webster

And the end of all our exploring
Will be to arrive where we started
And know the place for the first time.
—T. S. Eliot

The winter of 1861-62 was not a period of famine in China, so the impetus to leave was not great. Additional recruitment depots had been established in Canton/Hangshai, Swatow, and Amoy. In order to fill the vessels, the British officials combined people from these different regions onto each ship, not realizing their incompatibility. At the same time, there were private agencies in Hong Kong and China competing for workers to be sent to Cuba, California, and Peru. To the Europeans, China was viewed merely as an impoverished, overpopulated source for unskilled labour. Little concern was shown for the vast cultural and language differences. The British assessed the nature of the Chinese people as capable of surviving tropical conditions and of being hardy, industrious and ambitious. The reality of the situation was that those who were recruited for the purpose of emigrating had no idea of the implications of their actions. Many were people who had been displaced from their homes during bloody conflict, or who were just part of the marginal population.

— Helen Atteck & Philip Atteck, *Stress of Weather*

...in British Guiana, a number of individual Chinese families... had achieved prominence by the last quarter of the nineteenth century, most of them not only merchants but also large plantation owners. Among them was the family of John Ho-a-Shoo (1852-1906), who came with the Corona in 1874 and ten to fifteen years later was a sugar estate owner and prominent merchant (Ho-a-Shoo Ltd.) with several businesses in both the sugar-bearing and gold-mining areas of the colony. Three of his children studied at the University of Edinburgh in the 1900s and 1910s, two of them medicine and a third agriculture. One – a girl – Asin – became a Fellow of the Royal College of Surgeons, and eventually settled in Hong Kong in 1915. Another family of merchants and estate owners was that of David

Ewing-Chow, whose father arrived on the Dora in 1860 and whose two sons were in 1915 studying in England, one a law student at Cambridge, the other a medical student at Edinburgh. One of Georgetown's leading jewellers, based on Lombard Street, was M. U. Hing, whose grandfather had lost all his possessions in China, a victim of the Taiping Rebellion, and whose father, Wu A Hing had migrated to British Guiana as a mere boy on the Chapman in 1861. The most famous figure in 1915 was the Chinese empire builder Wong Yan-Sau (also known as Even Wong) who came to British Guiana at the age of ten with his parents on the Dartmouth in 1879. By 1915, he was one of the wealthiest colonists in British Guiana, owner of the Omai goldmines in Essequibo and several thousands of acres of plantations in East Coast, Demerara and Essequibo, growing sugar, cocoa, coffee, rubber, coconuts, and timber... he was a merchant and landlord of several businesses and properties in Georgetown and in the rural areas. He was also connected with the gold and diamond industries... owner and possessor of several sawmills, shareholder in many companies in Georgetown, and owner of several racehorses as well as a number of brood-mares. In 1915, one of his children was a student of civil engineering at Bristol University in England.

— Walton Look Lai, *Indentured Labor, Caribbean Sugar*

THE OLD LADY

Her name was Clarice Chung but in Canefield, Berbice, everyone called her *The Old Lady*, even her own children. *The Old Lady* could have meant any old lady, for there were many old ladies in Canefield, but there were no other *Chinese* old ladies. When they called her *The Old Lady,* they emphasised *old*, though when she came to live in Canefield in 1923 she was only fifty, and when she died there in 1946 she was seventy-three, not so very old at all. It was her Chineseness that made her seem old, to the point of being *ancient,* like China, and this is why the title stuck to her. She knew this and the awe it excited in people, so it pleased her to be called *The Old Lady*.

For twenty-three years, she sat in her shop in Canefield in the same spot, behind the counter, where she guarded the money drawer. She hardly moved except to open and close the drawer. She rarely spoke to customers, only to her three children, Norma, Frederick and Harold, who worked in the shop and bakery daily, obeying her commands and serving the customers. She did not speak to the customers other than when she had to, but she observed them closely; she spoke to them to let them know that her shop was not there to dispense charity, and they must pay the price she demanded for her goods. No one ever disputed the prices, or asked for discounts. They learned not to go to her shop for any other reason but to make a purchase – not for companionship or conversation or to shelter from the sun or rain. If a small group of men or women or children gathered in the shop to gossip, she ordered them to leave: "Gwan! Go way! Get out me shop!"

It was a shock when she broke her silence, as if a statue had suddenly come to life; they were so used to seeing her sitting very still, white as chalk and dressed in her black Chinese silk pyjamas, with one hand resting on the money drawer. Children rarely came across any actual dumb people in Canefield, so they came to think of *The Old Lady* as a dumb person. When she suddenly shrieked at them, waving her arms to shoo them away, it was terrifying, as if a corpse had risen from one of the graves in the churchyard to pursue them, a popular nightmare of theirs. Children did not like her and grew up to think of *The Old Lady* as a witch or devil.

Many years later, near the end of the twentieth century, these same children, those who were still in Guyana, now themselves nearing old age, were reluctant to speak to Joan Wong, Clarice Chung's granddaughter, who had returned to Canefield to research Clarice's history. They were reluctant because they had nothing good to say about her grandmother who had come to British Guiana in 1879, on the last ship to bring Chinese people to the colony.

FREDERICK WONG IN LOVE

In Canefield's only cinema, the *Tajmahal,* they showed the movies of Hollywood's golden era. Clarice noticed that after he saw these movies, the elder of her sons, Frederick, would use the word "love". It was his favourite word. Since he was a boy, he loved to watch Hollywood movies. He idolized the female film stars and would say how much he was in love with them. He collected their photos and pasted them on the walls of the shop with their names written plain for all to see – Claudette Colbert, Jane Wyman, Joan Crawford, and Rita Hayworth. Clarice often caught him staring at their photos with a dreamy expression. When she looked at Frederick's photos she called them *gweilos*, meaning *white ghosts*, and spat in contempt at their big bosoms and painted faces, with lipstick red like blood. They made her swear in Chinese, "Si!"

When he said he was in love with them, Clarice knew exactly what that meant. She thought that when your children talked about sex, it was time for them to marry. In Canefield, it was easy for her two sons, Frederick and Harold, to get sex, because they were shopkeepers. From the time they became teenagers in long pants, the women started to sweet talk them into giving them free groceries and joke that they would give them sex in return. Some women said they were only joking, but Clarice saw when Harold began taking women to the bottomhouse, the four-foot high space under the floorboards, where they stored

11

planks of wood, old furniture, empty oil drums and other rubbish. She gave him condoms and warned him not to make the women pregnant. When he reappeared from under the shop, she would check for discarded condoms among the rats, centipedes and cockroaches. If there were none, she would have it out with him in the shop so everyone could hear and he would be shamed into using the condoms.

One day, when she was reprimanding Harold, he lost his temper, ran to the kitchen for a cleaver and threatened to chop her. It was the first time she saw him in such a rage. The shop was full of customers but he did not care. He threatened to chop off her head, cut her into small pieces and throw her body parts into the canal. He chopped at the wooden counter, sending the splinters flying, leaving deep cuts. He swung the cleaver in the air, and rushed towards her. His face was red and swollen, he was bathed in sweat. She wailed and raised her arms to protect herself. The women in the shop shrieked in terror, and begged the men to disarm Harold, but he charged at them with the cleaver raised. In the mayhem and panic, Frederick shrank into a corner where he crouched and wept in fear. Seeing his older brother weeping brought Harold to his senses and he went to Frederick and handed him the cleaver, reassuring him that he would never hurt him, only *she,* he said, pointing to their mother who sat slumped in shock against the money drawer. The commotion brought their older sister Norma from the kitchen. She had watched in horror Harold's violent display.

Afterwards, there was silence between them, and business returned to normal, and the incident was never mentioned again, by the family or the customers.

This was not the only silence. There was also little

mention of the child, Doris, whom her oldest daughter Norma had conceived in her teens for an Indian man. Norma had been sent away to New Forest, where the child lived with her father. They also kept hidden away Clarice's younger daughter, Anna, who was an epileptic. Her fits were so severe she would foam at the mouth, collapse and shake violently; then her siblings would tie her with ropes and lock her away. Anna's fits, Norma's child and Harold's rage were kept out of sight so the family could give the impression they were living quiet, industrious, virtuous lives.

Not long after Harold's rampage, Clarice received a letter from her cousin in Georgetown, the doctor, Elizabeth Chung. Elizabeth told her that her laundress, Susan Leo, was looking for a husband for her daughter, Mary, and would like to come to Canefield to make a match with Frederick. The letter came when Clarice was thinking that something was needed to give stability to her family, and getting Frederick and Harold married might be just the thing. Frederick was really getting a little long in the tooth not to be married, and it disturbed her to see Harold having sex with all kinds of women. Harold already had a son with a black girl, Cordelia Patterson, conceived when she was working as their servant. One day, her belly started to grow, and then her mother came to the shop to tell Clarice that Harold was the father. Harold denied it and Clarice backed him up. All through her pregnancy, and after she had the baby, a boy she called Winston, Cordelia would come to the shop and sit there waiting to be given the recognition she wanted. In future years, when anyone asked the boy his name, he said "Winston Wong". The customers understood very well that by her silence Clarice was denying that the boy was related to her. Day after day, Cordelia and

Winston would sit in the shop in the corner on the long bench used by customers, behind the glass case where bread and cheese were displayed. Clarice sat on the other side of the glass case. She could see mother and child clearly but pretended she couldn't. She could see that the little boy bore a resemblance to Harold. His eyes were almond-shaped, with long eyelashes and his mouth was small like Harold's, with round lips. Although his mother's skin was dark, Winston's skin was a very light brown, like toffee. Sometimes Clarice was tempted to soften her heart and give the boy a drink or cake, but she knew that the slightest weakness on her part would be taken as an acknowledgement that Harold was his father. Sometimes she even felt sorry for the mother too, but hardened her heart against her. She was certain that Cordelia wanted to be given goods from the shop for nothing and Clarice was determined that she would never get that. With just one exception, it was only Clarice's silence that Cordelia ever knew.

Sometimes customers in the shop would try to make Clarice speak by greeting her, "Good morning, Miss Chung!", "How you do, Miss Chung?", but she refused to respond. To excuse her, Frederick would even tell people, "She can only talk Chinese", though he knew that while she rarely spoke English, she could communicate perfectly well in Creole. He would remind them she came from China, though he couldn't be sure if that was true. One thing was certain, if you told people she came from China and she spoke Chinese, they became overawed and kept their distance. Who knew what was true? Only Clarice knew the truth, and in Canefield she remained a mystery so no one could take advantage of her. This was her biggest fear. She'd taken Cordelia in when she was thirteen years old, given her food, clothes, and shelter; all she had to do in return was cook, sweep, and wash clothes. It injured Clarice

14

to think that Cordelia was trying to bring disgrace on her. But just once, when they were sitting in silence in the shop, her sense of injury and betrayal so overwhelmed her that she began to complain bitterly to Cordelia about the injuries she had borne in her life.

Cordelia was so used to Clarice's silence that the sound of her voice made her jump with fright, but she listened keenly, trying to understand what Clarice was saying. It was difficult because to tell her story Clarice mixed Creole with some random Mandarin words she had brought from China. She spoke some Hakka, too, and this was also mixed in. It was in this eclectic language that Clarice told Cordelia every single thing about herself, about her memories of the China she left in December 1878. It was a language filled with grief, bewilderment and anger that this was how she had ended up – a Chinese person, whom no one understood, on a remote, poverty-stricken sugar estate in British Guiana, far from the homeland she would never see again. When she arrived on a ship, the *Admiral*, in 1879, she and her family had to stop speaking their language, had to stop being Chinese because people laughed at them.

People thought she did not remember China, but she did. Her children would tell people, "She come from China long long time ago, but she don't remember nothing, she don't remember, she forget", but she remembered everything, and she told Cordelia Patterson about her memories, her feelings of loss, of having to become a different person in British Guiana, a person whose children were not real Chinese, and would never be real Chinese because they did not speak Chinese or have any Chinese culture. As she spoke, she looked at the small boy who was supposed to be her grandchild, the little black boy with Chinese eyes. She knew he did not understand what she was saying, but she wanted him to remember the day

15

his Chinese grandmother opened her mouth and spoke her whole history. It was the first and last time she ever did this. She talked so much that day it wore her out, and made her wonder why she'd done it.

Frederick overheard all this because he was sitting in the small room behind the shop doing the accounts. He, too, did not understand all she was saying, only the Creole parts, but it shocked him to hear her pouring out her heart to Cordelia Patterson, and he wondered what had prompted her to do it. It so mystified him he came into the shop to stand beside his mother, gazing at her in surprise and waiting for her to speak to him because he felt that she owed him an explanation. He found his mother's pain unbearable; it reminded him of how unhappy her brooding had made him as a little boy, and he could see that it was making little Winston unhappy too, so he gave him a lollipop and Cordelia a bottle of chilled malted milk. It brought smiles to their faces, and made Frederick smile too, but Clarice grimaced, to show Frederick she was not happy with his generosity.

It was at this moment that she gave Frederick the letter she had received from Elizabeth Chung and he read its contents to her. He had gone to school and learned to read and write; she relied on him to do this for her. When he handed her back the letter, she put it in the money drawer and declared that it was time for him to get married before he too "get baby with black and coolie people".

She told Frederick to write to Elizabeth Chung and ask her to send a photo of the girl they wanted to make a match with; it was time for him to get married and have children legally. For the sake of peace, Frederick never argued with his mother, so he wrote the letter and asked Elizabeth Chung to send a photograph of his prospective marriage match.

When the photo arrived of Mary Leo, Frederick fell in love with her image instantly and decided he would marry her. He thought she looked like Jane Wyman, his favourite Hollywood pin-up, and he put the photo next to Jane's, above his bed. He told his mother he did not need to meet Mary Leo to be sure he wanted to marry her, but she told him not to be so foolish; it was imperative he meet her first, so she chose a date for Susan Leo to visit them with her daughter, Mary.

Norma was not happy. She tried to dissuade her mother from permitting Frederick to marry and gave many reasons: they could not afford a wedding; the place was too small with just a bedroom and kitchen behind the shop; there was no room for anyone else. Norma wept and begged her mother not to let Frederick bring a new wife to their home. She flew into a rage, pulled down the photo of Mary and tore it into shreds and threw them down the latrine.

Clarice ignored her, knowing exactly why Norma was behaving like this. She was afraid she would have to move out, and go to live in New Forest with Henry Singh and Doris. He was always begging Norma to live with them, but Norma refused because she was ashamed she'd had a child with an Indian man; she had always hoped to marry a Chinese man. Before conceiving the child, she used to beg her mother to find her a husband from Hong Kong, saying she would only leave her mother's home to live with a real Chinese husband.

THE MARRIAGE MATCH

On the day of the marriage match, Susan Leo arrived with not one, but four daughters. It was midday, the sun was high up in a bright blue sky; it was very hot; there was no breeze. Clarice was sitting in her usual place, near the money drawer, fanning herself. There were no customers in the shop. At this time of day, the only people outdoors were the field workers. Other people would wait for the day to cool before they came to the shop. Not even the stray dogs moved on such a hot day.

Into this stillness, Susan Leo and her daughters appeared suddenly, like apparitions. Clarice had assumed that Elizabeth Chung would choose a Chinese family for a marriage match, but as soon as she saw them, she knew the girls were not pure Chinese, that they were mixed with another race. Susan Leo looked Chinese but she was dressed like an East Indian; she was wearing the short white organza ornhi that Indian women wore on formal occasions, along with a nose ring, gold bangles, earrings and necklaces. She was such a small, skinny woman she looked weighed down by her jewellery. Her daughters were well built, with big bosoms; they looked alert, healthy and well-fed while their mother looked starved and tired. One thing was certain, the daughters were a good-looking bunch, all of them dolled up. And even in her middle age, you could see that Susan Leo was still a pretty woman. There was an air of glamour about her. Her clothes were immaculately laundered. The ornhi was a dazzling, pristine white; it had been washed and ironed meticulously, like her pale cream floral dress.

Clarice was dressed as usual in one of her many thickly-woven black Chinese silk pyjamas, a uniform that made her sweat. While Clarice looked like a heavy black statue, Susan Leo radiated softness and airiness.

Clarice did not offer them anything to drink. They had to understand from the start that she did not give anything away for free. If they wanted food and drink from the shop, they had to pay for it. Susan's daughters were hungry and thirsty; they were asking their mother to buy them food and drink but she ignored them. Clarice concluded they were poor and could not afford it.

Susan introduced herself politely, "Good day, Miss Chung. I is the same Susan Leo that you are expecting, and this here is my daughter, Mary, who I bring today to make a marriage match with your son."

Clarice demanded to know if Mary was pure Chinese.

"No, Miss Chung, she is only half Chinee and half Indian. All my girls here have the same Indian father, James Abdul, but he lef' me and I had was to raise me children by meself." Susan was too proud to tell Clarice that, in fact, James Abdul had abandoned her with six children to look after while he took an Indian wife who bore him more children. In her struggle to raise her six children, two had died. Her eyes were full of pain and sorrow when she spoke about James Abdul and remembered the death of her infant son, Ishmael, and one daughter, Gwendolyn, when she was only ten years old. She struggled to hold back the tears. Her daughters knew this, and they held hands and formed a half-circle around their mother.

Clarice said: "You shoulda know better, you too damn stupid to get pickney with coolie man. You too damn stupid!" Then she asked, "Which one is Mary?"

19

Of the four girls, Mary looked the strongest. If she really was as strong as she looked, she would make a good worker; she would be able to work in the shop, and also do the cooking, cleaning and washing clothes.

Clarice asked Susan if Mary could work hard.

"Oh yes, Miss Chung, she train to do everything. I send her to live with my black friend Evadne Williams for four years. Evadne was a servant for rich white an Chinee people in Georgetown, she get good training with them, and she teach Mary good how to do housework, to cook, clean and do laundry how white people like it. She train her to be a good servant."

"You give black people you own pickney?" Clarice snapped. "What kinda Chinee is you? You get plenty pickney with coolie man; he lef' you an you give 'way you pickney to black people? You ain't no prapa Chinee! You come from China? I come from China, I is real Chinee. Me husband, John Wong, was Chinee too; he Hakka, but he family come from China. I get four pickney with he; all me pickney is Chinee; you pickney ain't Chinee, you pickney is half-breed. I prefer me pickney married real Chinee."

It seemed that Clarice was on the verge of rejecting Mary Leo, but Frederick, standing in the room behind the shop, had heard everything. He came forward to reveal himself. He introduced himself to Mary, and shook her hand.

"I like Mary," he told his mother, "I sure I want she." Then Frederick offered all the Leo family iced drinks and cakes for which they were very grateful.

Susan explained, "Thank you, sir. We catch train five o clock dis morning, we only drink one cup tea. Whole morning we ain't eat or drink nothing. We hungry and thirsty so bad. T'ank you, sir."

He said, "Don't call me sir. I is Frederick, the person you come to make match for. I is the marriage match."

"If I had money," Susan said, "I would pay you for the drinks and cake, sir, but I don't have money today."

All the Leos smiled at Frederick. All morning they had worried about whether Mary would be accepted. Their lives had been difficult, but Mary's was the most difficult, least cared for of all, and her sisters dearly wanted her to find her a good man to marry, who would take care of her. Frederick's kindness came as an enormous relief.

Clarice did not want Susan Leo and her daughters to think that she was as soft-hearted as her son, so she spoke severely, to show that they could not take advantage of her.

"You know who is my family? You know who is Arnold Chung? You hear 'bout he? He was me father brother, he was me uncle, richest Chinee man in Georgetown. He an my father George Chung build governor house in Main Street; he build plenty big-shot house in Georgetown. All dem nice nice house you see in Queenstown an Kingston, where all dem big shot people live, me uncle an father build. You ever hear 'bout Chief Justice Joseph Chung? That is he son! He other son is Jacob Chung; he was rich rich rich, he had plenty gold mine. All their pickney go to England and study. All turn doctor and lawyer. He third son is James Chung, he got plenty property and plenty store in Georgetown. Di doctor, Elizabeth Chung, dat send you here, she is he daughter; she study medicine in England. So don' tink I is like you. I is better than you. I is real Chinee, I ain't no Hakka Chinee. Me and me family was last real Chinee come he' 'pon the last ship that bring Chinee people. We come here fresh fresh, pure Chinee, we was not like allyou Hakka Chinee that come here long time and get chil'ren with black an' coolie people, eat black and coolie food an' forget China. I ain't forget China; it still in me brain, not like all you Hakka that stay here so long you can't remember nothing. I come 'pon last ship from China, so I remember China. I

21

is still like how I was when I come from China. I is a real Chinee; you no real Chinee."

Susan Leo knew that the Chungs were the most important and richest Chinese family in the country and she nodded in agreement while Clarice listed their accomplishments. When she finished, Clarice pointed to herself. "I is Chung too, I is Clarice Chung! Me name change to Wong when I married John Wong; he was Hakka Chinee, but I ain't no Hakka, me Chung family was Punti, so I keep me Chung name. I tell people call me 'Miss Chung'. We Punti had land and property in China. Dem Hakka people dat come here din have nothing, nothing! Me family was royal Chinee! Emperor Chengzong was me family! Dey send we here to build this country! In Hong Kong, *Xian Gang*, we build plenty big property; that is why they send we here, to build this country!"

She pointed to Susan Leo and demanded to know if her family were Hakka or Punti, and if they had money.

Susan Leo responded timidly, "No, Miss Chung, my family din' have no money at all, dey was poor Hakka people. Me parents come 'pon the boat from China an had me here, but they die an lef me so I din born in China like you. I born here. I was only four years old when they die an lef me, an I had was to go in the orphanage with the nuns, but Chinee people take me in an care for me, and in return I work for them. I clean their house, wash their clothes and cook fo' them, an that is how come I survive and manage. I work as servant and laundress for rich Chinee an white people, an I run a fruit an' grain stall in Stabroek market. That is how I live, Miss Chung. I don't have money. I have to work hard for what money I get; is a hard life I have, Miss Chung, to feed me and my children. I din have rich family like you. Is by the grace of god I meet Mrs. Li and her mother-in-law, Dr. Chung, and they help me out. Mrs. Li foster two of my girls, Jean and Sally, she take them in her home an look after them, she send them to convent school to learn to read and write. She and Dr. Chung give them clothes, books and toys. They help me."

Clarice grumbled, "Well you see me here? I ain't going help you like me rich family. I poor like you. I gat to work hard in dis shop, me and my chil'ren. An if you daughter goin married and live he' she gat to wuk hard. Me shop ain't no Dharam Sala. You understand?"

Susan nodded and promised that Mary would work hard, after she married Frederick.

"So if you don' have money, who you expec' to pay fo' this wedding?" Clarice snapped. "Me? I ain't paying for this wedding! You have to pay your share!"

Frederick intervened, telling Susan she did not have to pay anything for the wedding. He said he would like the wedding to take place in a month, and he set a date.

"Thank you, sir," Susan said, bowing to him, and turned as if to leave, but Clarice signalled her to stay and sit down on the bench with her daughters.

Clarice said, "I got two son, the nex' one is Harold. I want wife fo' he too. You got three more daughter. What about one a dem married Harold?" Harold was at work in the backyard, baking cakes in the oven. She told Frederick to fetch him. Harold appeared, bathed in sweat in his white string vest and khaki short pants. Clarice pointed to Mary and told him, "We make match for Frederick wid she. She name Mary. Frederick want married she next month. Look, she gat three sister. You want married one a dem? Which wan you want?"

Harold pointed to the smallest of the girls, Lily, who was so startled she gasped and cried out, "Oh Gawd! Me?"

Susan was also surprised but she was glad to think she could marry off two of her daughters so easily, into a family that was prospering, where they would be taken care of. With two mouths less to feed, life would be a little easier, so it was to all their advantage to accept a marriage match for both Mary and Lily, so she nodded enthusiastically, and her daughters, seeing her agree, also nodded their assent, though they felt some grief to think that they were going to be split up.

Clarice felt pleased to have accomplished two marriage matches so quickly and easily. Once they came to live in her household, the two sisters would be extra pairs of hands to help in the house and the shop. With her epilepsy, Anna was no help at all, she was just a burden. With her brothers getting two wives, there would be less room, and this would make Norma finally move out and go and live with Henry Singh in New Forest where he had a nice, big cottage. Norma spent many weekends there with him and Doris, and sometimes she took Anna. It would be a good arrangement to be rid of Anna for longer periods. Clarice had not seen it as clearly as she saw it now, and her mind raced around trying to think whether there was more she could get out of this situation.

Everyone was smiling now, except Clarice. She did not want to leave anything to chance; experience had taught her not to allow fate to control her destiny. Fate had torn her away from China when she was just a small child. Susan Leo called herself an orphan, as if only she knew what that felt like, but Clarice knew what it felt like too. She'd felt like an orphan when she left China, she'd felt like an orphan during the journey to British Guiana, and she felt even more like an orphan in British Guiana. Her parents had not died when she was young like Sarah Leo's; they saw her married to John Wong before they died, but she'd still felt like an orphan all her life. No one could really understand or know who she was, even her own children. The most painful thing about coming to British Guiana was never to be understood. She had come with her father and his four brothers. The eldest brother was Cheung Chang Bo, who later changed his name to Arnold Chung; his wife, Jun, changed her name to Margaret Chung. They came with their two sons, Ming (who became Joseph Chung) and Ling (who became Jacob Chung). Her father was the second of the brothers. His name was Cheung Mu Bo but he changed it to George Chung. Her mother's name was She, but she changed it to Sheila. The third brother was Cheung Sam Bak; he became Peter Chung and married a Hakka woman, Gloria Lee. The youngest brother, Cheung Wan Bak, became Bertram Chung; he, too, married a Hakka, Henrietta Chin.

When they arrived, everyone laughed at them. They laughed at their Chinese clothes, they laughed at the Chinese they spoke, they laughed at the difficulties they experienced trying to understand English and Creole; they laughed even more when they tried to speak it. They were like animals in a zoo, to be pointed and stared at. Clarice just wanted to be invisible and silent and spent her childhood in British Guiana trying to pretend she did not exist, trying not to speak because she found life in British Guiana incomprehensible and confusing. They had not been poor in China – they were well off because the Cheung brothers were builders who always had plenty of work and could provide for their families – but in British Guiana they became poor. As soon as they came off the boat, they were put to live in wooden huts on Soesdyke estate, where the Cheung brothers became labourers like the blacks and coolies. They had to work in the open in the canefields exposed to the blazing sun and driving rain, and in the sugar factory where there were many accidents that left people permanently injured, even limbless. The Cheungs had never experienced such terrible hardship and poverty. They barely earned enough to feed and look after their families, but they were determined to improve their lives, especially the eldest brother, Arnold Chung, who through sheer determination drove himself and his brothers to work hard, leave the estate, and go into various businesses. They became farmers who used their produce to open restaurants, groceries and bakeries, then branch into other businesses. They educated their children and sent them abroad to study, to return to the country in important professions. They became a prominent middle-class clan and Clarice liked to bask in the glory of their achievements, though she herself was just a humble shopkeeper. So when she heard Sarah Leo or anyone else relate how difficult their life had been, she understood them, but she had learned not to show she felt sorry for anyone. She did not understand where Frederick got his soft nature from, perhaps from his father, John Wong, who got it from his own father, William Wong, who helped the Chungs when they first arrived on Soesdyke estate. He owned a grocery then; he had heard about the arrival of this new Chinese family, and he knew how difficult it was to start from scratch. His own Hakka family, and many others, had endured that terrible struggle, starting life on a sugar estate, living in a wooden hut with no furniture, no beds to sleep on, nothing to cook food with, and no money to buy anything, so he took it on himself to get a horse and cart, and load it with the things the Chungs needed, including food. He gave it all to them for nothing, though the Chung brothers insisted they would gradually pay him back for everything he had given them, and they did. So, it must have been from William Wong, her father-in-law, that Frederick had inherited his soft-heartedess. He felt sorry for people too easily; if someone was too poor to pay for

groceries and they begged him for mercy, he gave it immediately, he gave them food without stopping to count the
cost. As far as she was concerned, running a shop you had to
count the cost of everything, but not Frederick, he would
give away the whole shop to poor people if he could. She saw
how he looked at Mary Leo lovingly; she saw that he felt pity
for Susan Leo and her daughters, but she was not going to let
him give away everything she had. The Leo family were not
going to become a burden but a help to her. Susan Leo had
two more daughters to find husbands for – and she, Clarice,
would find a way to turn it to her advantage.

DOUBLE WEDDING.

Susan and her daughters returned to Georgetown. The next day, she went straight to Elizabeth Chung to give her the good news that two marriage matches were made. Elizabeth knew that Susan could not afford the expense of the wedding and promised that she and Elaine Li would provide the two girls with wedding dresses; she would get her own seamstress to sew them; she would also give Susan a bonus of fifty dollars to help her with the wedding.

While the Leos were back in Georgetown, Clarice Chung pursued her own plan to get the rest of the Leo women married off. It occurred to her that she could get Jean Leo married off to her dentist, Joe Persaud. She owed him plenty dollars for pulling her family's teeth. In exchange for finding him a wife, she would ask him to cancel that debt. Joe Persaud was a big strapping fellow with a mouth full of gold teeth who spent his days travelling all over Berbice, pulling teeth. He carried a doctor's bag, full of dental implements – needles, anaesthetic, pliers , and moulds for making false teeth. She did not like him – he was the biggest womaniser in Berbice – but his dental bills were a big expense. In exchange for a wife, she could demand cut-price work from him in future and cancellation of her debts. When Clarice sent for him, he came at once, thinking she needed him to pull a tooth. Instead, she asked him,

"When you going get married, Joe Persaud?"

"Me? Married? Who tell you I want get married? Marriage is worries. I don't want no wife to eat up me money. I still young, I still like to sport. I ain't ready for wife and pickney."

"You is a no-good, whoring, drunk coolie. You like too much woman. You need wife and pickney to make you settle down and behave."

"You got a nice Chinee girl for me? A beautiful Chinee girl from Hong Kong?"

"Don' talk no stupidness. You tink any Hong Kong Chinee girl would marry ugly, black-skin, drunk-man coolie like you? I find marriage match fo' Frederick and Harold; two girl from Georgetown; they is half-Indian, half-Chinee; they got two more sister. I can get one fo' you; she name Jean. You want she? She look like flim star, she comin he' next month fo the wedding. Come and see if you want married she, but you got to cancel me debt if you want she, and charge me half price from now."

Once she got Joe Persaud interested, Clarice focused next on Jimmy Chu, a Chinese youth she was fond of, who was a skilful carpenter and mechanic. Jimmy could turn his hand to anything to make a living. He did all her carpentry work. He could build a house single-handed. In exchange for a wife, he must build a new house in her yard for Harold to live with Lily. Long ago she would have liked Jimmy as a husband for Norma, but that was not to be. If only Norma had wanted Jimmy Chu, he was such a beautiful Chinee man, with wavy black hair, milky-white skin and heart-shaped pink lips. He and Norma would have made beautiful Chinee children with white skin. Well, if she could not get him for Norma, she might as well get him for the youngest Leo woman, Sally. With Sally married to Jimmy, and her sisters married to her sons, the couples would be like one big clan living in the same yard, and all of them would work for her. Jimmy would do all her building work for free. Matchmaking was a business that would profit her in the long run. With the Leo women doing the housework, she would save money on employing servants. By marrying them to her dentist and carpenter, she would get big discounts and save more money. She sent for Jimmy to tell him she found him a marriage match and he must come to the wedding to meet her. She also made it clear that whilst she would provide the materials, she would expect him, in exchange, to build a new house for her, and he agreed.

THE CREOLE WEDDING

On the day of the wedding, the Leos travelled again to Canefield. They left Georgetown in joyful spirits, so excited they did not sleep the night before, and woke very early to bathe and pack their wedding dresses into suitcases given to them by Elizabeth Chung and Helen Li.

All their lives they had lived in the confines of Georgetown; they were not used to the wide open spaces they saw from the windows of the train as it sped along the East Coast of Demerara into the West Coast of Berbice. They leaned out the windows to feel the wind in the roots of their hair and catch the leaves of the banana trees that grew beside the railway line. They were so excited, Susan had to smack them into calming down. With the fifty dollars Dr. Chung had given her, she indulged the girls when the train stopped at Mahaica where hucksters paraded up and down the platform with trays of fruit and food. The first time they had travelled to Berbice, she did not have money to buy them food, but now she bought fried fish with pepper sauce in long fresh loaves of bread, a big bunch of fig bananas, and chilled bottles of soft drinks. They hugged their mother in gratitude, and jumped around with happiness. She pushed them away and snapped, "You is big women now, you going married today. Behave!"

When they arrived at the shop, Clarice showed them to the backyard where Frederick, Harold, Norma, Anna, Joe Persaud and Jimmy Chung were waiting, seated on hired chairs that were set out in a circle all around the yard.

31

"Go inside and change you clothes," Clarice instructed, pointing to the back of the shop where a landing led to the bedroom that was shared by the entire family. Norma led the way to the bedroom and showed them the bed shared by Frederick and Harold, and told Mary and Lily to put their things there, but they were not to touch the bed she shared with Clarice and Anna.

It did not surprise the Leos to see that the whole family shared one bedroom since it was the same arrangement back in their rented room in Albuoystown. They grew up sharing a bed, all four of them, until Jean and Sally went to live with Elaine Li, but whenever they returned to live with their mother, it was sharing again. Norma and Anna did not give them any privacy while they changed; they watched resentfully as the Leo sisters helped each other into their pretty wedding dresses. Norma and Anna Wong, like their mother, were dressed drearily in black Chinese silk pyjamas.

When Mary and Lily returned to the yard in white wedding dresses, Clarice gave them a bitter look of disapproval and launched into a diatribe. She declared that in China, brides wore red; Chinese people wore white only for funerals. She talked about her own wedding many years ago, how it was a real Chinese wedding, how she wore red, like a real Chinese bride. She told them they ate Chinese food at her wedding, but she could not afford to send for a Chinese cook from Georgetown so they would eat no Chinese food today; she expected them to cook the food or else they would not eat.

Susan readily agreed to do the cooking, and pointed to the chickens in the coop, offering to kill, feather and curry two of them while Jean and Sally cooked the roti.

"And you going pay fo the food?" Clarice asked.

Susan drew some crumpled notes from her pocket and handed them to Clarice who took them quickly, and pointed to the kitchen. Susan went there, filled the largest pots with water and put them on to boil while Norma followed, watching her suspiciously. Mary asked Frederick for flour, oil, salt, curry powder and ghee. Eager to please her, he quickly fetched these from the shop. Jimmy Chu was already attracted to Sally and wanted to impress her, so he collected two chickens from the coop, and holding them over a bowl while they squawked and struggled to escape, expertly sliced off their heads and collected the blood in a bowl, declaring that the blood was tasty when added to curry sauce. Frederick brought him two buckets of boiling water and the now dead chickens were pushed in and held down to soak in preparation for plucking their feathers, a task Jimmy undertook with the same skill with which he sliced off their heads.

Clarice disapproved of how ready Frederick was to supply the Leos with goods from her shop without asking her permission. She warned him not to do it again. She told Susan she was going to give her the bill for everything, including the two chickens. Jimmy Chu intervened and promised Clarice he would pay for the chickens. He smiled at Sally, then whispered to Clarice that he would marry her.

Joe Persaud was reluctant to commit himself as quickly as Jimmy, and held back, but he liked the look of Jean because she was the prettiest of the sisters with her curly, glossy black hair, flashing grey-green eyes, and shining fake jewellery. Clarice was pleased to see that her matchmaking for Jimmy Chu was going to bear fruit; she looked forward to him building her new house, for which she would not have to pay him a penny for the labour. She voiced this thought openly, for all to hear, then asked Joe Persaud loudly whether he was going to take Jean Leo for a wife, then stop charging her for his dental services.

Soon, the delicious scent of Susan's cooking filled the yard and everyone ate contentedly from steaming plates of chicken curry, rice and roti, all except Clarice and her two daughters, who said they did not want coolie food and instead ate their own chinee cake and mauby from the shop.

After the meal, they formed a procession and walked to the Anglican church from where the bells' clear sound seemed to spread everywhere, like the light, as far as the distant horizons.

Mary felt alone, though her mother and sisters walked beside her, with her new husband and his family surrounding them. When, for four years, she lived with Evadne Williams in Charlestown, she used to miss her family. Now, with Frederick's family, her family was doubled. She had always mourned not having a father, but now she was going to have two mothers, two more sisters and the brother she'd never had since her only brother died when he was a baby. What was there to regret? Perhaps it was the vast Berbice sky, so deep above her, that made her feel small. Back in Georgetown, where she had lived all the nineteen years of her life, the sky never looked so high and deep. There, the horizons were never so far away; buildings always surrounded you, and the paved roads made your feet feel firm underfoot. There was too much open space here in Berbice, like a big hole ready to swallow you. But then from the church came the voices of people singing hymns. It was a hymn she knew and loved, so she sang along quietly, to calm her nerves:

> There is a green hill far away,
> Without a city wall,
> Where our dear Lord was crucified,
> Who died to save us all.

Oh, dearly, dearly has He loved,
And died our sins to bear;
We trust in His redeeming blood,
And life eternal share.

We may not know, we cannot tell,
What pains He had to bear;
But we believe it was for us
He hung and suffered there.

He died that we might be forgiven,
He died to make us good,
That we might from our sins be freed,
Saved by His precious blood.

There was no other good enough
To pay the price of sin,
He only could divine life give
And dwell Himself within.

The wide open spaces had made Mary feel she was falling
through space, but stepping inside the church stopped the
sensation of falling. The scent of incense, the sight of the
altar, the priest in his robes surrounded by his deacons and
choristers, the whole scene of worship, soothed her fears.
Her mother, always so poor, had given them away to
others, but one thing she did give them was the Roman
Catholic faith. She had all her children baptised and confirmed, and took them to Brickdam Cathedral every Sunday morning where high mass became their greatest con-
solation. Though this was an Anglican church and the
priest spoke in English, not Latin, it did not matter.

While the brides and their family participated in the
communion with the deepest sincerity, the Wong family

looked on in incomprehension because none of them were baptised or confirmed in the Christian church, though Arnold Chung used to claim that in Hong Kong, they were aristocratic Chinese Christians who came to British Guiana to convert the Hakkas to Christianity. Now here were his third generation descendants standing before the altar of an Anglican church on a sugar estate, struck dumb by the mysteries of the service, unable to participate in the rituals, while the Leos, whom they regarded as Hakka and creole inferiors, participated with the greatest sincerity, singing the Sanctus and Kyrie Eleison with deep passion, with tears in their eyes.

The Leos did not feel welcome or comfortable at the Wongs' shop, but here in the church they were at home, though Clarice had arranged a church wedding only because it was cheaper than a civil wedding at the town hall in New Amsterdam. The priest knew they were not Christians, but he agreed to perform the ceremony after the mass in the hope that the next generation of Wongs would join the church. He noticed with satisfaction how ardently the Leos participated; he would encourage the new brides to attend church, then perhaps their husbands and in-laws would follow.

Clarice noticed how the Leos were familiar with the service; how sincerely they sang, knelt and made the sign of the cross. She did not like the Christian religion; it was for black slaves, not her. She saw how the Leos knelt at the altar with black people and drank wine from the same cup. It repelled her to think of placing her lips on the same cup the black people sipped from and drink what the priest called the *blood of Christ*. It was like their obeah ceremonies where, she heard, they drank the raw blood of the animals they sacrificed. The Indian Kali Mai followers drank raw blood at their rituals, too. At nights, Clarice could hear the drumming and singing of the obeah and Kali Mai devotees on the estate; it kept her awake. In the shop, when the customers were angry with her, they threatened to get the obeah man or Kali pujari to put a curse on her, and when she fell ill or business was bad, she was certain it was because someone had put a bad spell on her.

The mass put the Leos in a good mood. All the way back to the shop, they hummed the Sanctus. Back in the yard, Frederick and Harold distributed iced mauby to everyone. Joe Persaud asked for beers, but Clarice told him to pay up first. Jimmy Chu paid for his beers, and when the two men had drunk enough, Clarice introduced them more formally to Jean and Sally Leo, and suggested they might marry them in the near future, then they too could come and live in Berbice, and be near their sisters. She told them Jimmy was going to build a big new house in the yard, where Harold would live with Lily; it would have plenty of room; they could come and stay with them sometimes. She told Susan, "You see how I treat you good? I find husband for all you pickney, an' I going give them brand new house."

There was a fruit cake for the couples to cut and distribute. Susan put her two pieces of cake in her pocket, but all the way back to Georgetown she felt at them so nervously that by the time they arrived home, the slices were just sandy crumbs, and though she was very hungry, she emptied her pocket into the gutter and went to bed feeling empty and worn out. In one single day she had given away all her daughters to Clarice Chung. Now, she had no more children, she was alone again, as she had been when she was four and her parents died and she became an orphan in Georgetown, passed from family to family to work as a servant for her keep. Now, approaching old age, she was like an orphan again.

While Susan Leo was mourning the loss of Mary and Lily, guessing that Clarice would treat them like servants, they were getting used to their first night on Canefield sugar estate. On their wedding night, they stayed up late on the landing with their husbands, while Clarice and her daughters turned off all the lights and went to bed early. It was so dark you could see nothing, but you could hear everything. The silence was as deep as the darkness and every sound came to you swiftly, borne by the breeze that blew continually at night across the wide open spaces. They could hear what they could not see: voices from the Indian families who lived in the two logies behind the shop, and the low growling from the machines in the factory across the canal. At night it sounded like the snores of a sleeping animal.

It was the first time the couples were alone together. Harold and Frederick decided they were not all going to sleep in one bed. Harold and Lily would sleep on the jute sacks of rice and split peas in the shop, and Frederick and Mary could have the bed to themselves, then the next night they would exchange places. Before they retired for the night, they took turns to bathe in the bathhouse at the bottom of the yard. Each couple took with them two buckets of water drawn from the roadside standpipe, a candle and towels, with one holding up the candle to light the darkness while the other soaped and rinsed. The women were too shy to appear naked and wore old dresses to bathe in. From her bed, Clarice heard them splashing and laughing in the bathhouse, and she could smell the perfume of the soap filling the yard. She heard Harold and Lily as they headed for the shop and settled down on the jute sacks and she heard when Frederick and Mary settled down in the bed next to hers. She could not resist speaking, and told them they were going to bed too late; the next day would be very busy in the shop; in future, they must go to bed earlier.

They ignored her and in the nights to come, the two couples enjoyed staying up late to sit on the landing to talk.

The morning after their wedding night, Clarice checked for condoms in the yard, to see if her sons had used them, but she found none.

That night, Clarice did not sleep; she was swamped by memories of her own Chinese wedding, long ago.

THE CHINESE WEDDING

In her mind she could see it all, as if she were watching it at the cinema. She could see herself young again, with John Wong when they fell in love, when he used to tow her on his bicycle around Georgetown. She used to stay with his parents while her mother went to work at her Uncle Arnold's house in Kingston. In those days, they were still living at Soesdyke sugar estate. Her father did not do as well as his brothers. He was left back on the sugar estate, still struggling and poor and her mother had to go out to work as a servant for his wealthy brother, Arnold Chung, in his big house in Kingston. Clarice did not like to go to Arnold Chung's house with her; she hated her cousin, Jacob, who used to torment her, so she went to stay with William Wong, who had helped them when they first came to British Guiana, who had remained her father's close friend. He had one son, John. When it was time for her to go and meet her mother in Kingston, John used to tow her there on his bicycle. She used to sit sideways on the bar, snuggled between his arms and legs. As he pedalled, his thighs brushed her hips and she could feel his breath on her neck. They would giggle self-consciously and try to get closer. She remembered how sometimes, he kissed her neck, then she would slap his face, scream in protest and threaten to complain to their parents. Their physical intimacy on these journeys was their secret, but her mother noticed that when Clarice arrived, she was blushing and coy, while John looked very happy and satisfied with himself. It was obvious to her they were in love, and she told her husband so. She told him it was time for Clarice to get married; she was not such a young woman – the problem had been finding a suitable husband for her – and though he was Hakka, they should propose a marriage match with John Wong. They discussed this openly, in front of her. Her father agreed that it was time for Clarice to marry, but he could not afford to pay for the wedding, unless his brother Arnold paid him in advance or lent him the money, so he went to Arnold Chung to ask for his help.

Arnold Chung had soon come to understand the English class system and how it had been adapted along racial lines in Georgetown. His ambition had been to climb it as rapidly as possible. At the top, like royalty and aristocrats, were the white expatriates who held the most powerful government positions and commanded the financial, mining and agricultural resources of the country. They were like lords of the realm, living in the grandest houses with armies of servants waiting on them. They installed only British-made goods in their homes – electric washing machines, the latest lavatory fittings, kitchens, vacuum cleaners, furniture, china, soft furnishings, and the electric cookers and ovens that were only available in shops where the English community shopped and the locals could only window-shop. The British upper classes in Georgetown were always travelling to Europe by boat and plane to holiday and shop. They sent away their children to boarding schools in England; their wives practised English upper-class etiquette that they imitated from British magazines; they dressed in the latest European and American fashions. At their parties, they drank from crystal glasses and ate from the finest bone china. They taught their servants to imitate the recipes of European cuisine.

On the edges of this group a few non-Europeans moved. There was an Indian family that dominated the legal profession, and another that owned a great deal of land; a Portuguese family, the Texeiras, who had a monopoly on the shipping industry, and among the paler Coloured families were those who dominated the upper reaches of the civil service. They lived in the best houses in the smartest areas such as Kingston and Queenstown and had their own exclusive clubs where they met to socialise and play sports. They raced to keep up with the whites, mimicking their lifestyle in every detail, wanting the latest Daimler or Morris cars from England, the latest Cadillac or Ford cars from America, wanting to furnish their homes like theirs, wear the same clothes, eat the same foods and send their children to Europe to be educated.

Arnold and Margaret Chung had long been determined to join this class, and they worked their way up until were wealthy enough to own a big house full of the latest luxury goods and be invited to the best parties. But Arnold was never content. No sooner had he achieved one ambition for himself and his children, he was pursuing another.

He had pursued the British governor until His Excellency promised to support him as a building contractor in Georgetown and help him get exclusive contracts for new government buildings, offices and schools. As the leader of the Chinese community in Georgetown, he had access to a ready labour force, one that he exploited ruthlessly, underpaying and overworking them. In the beginning this had included his brothers who worked with him as partners, but were not treated as equals. While he and his family had lived in comfort in Kingstown, his brothers were left in Soesdyke, living like peasants, until two of them could afford to come to Georgetown, though at first only to rent houses in Charlestown, a slum area that came to be known as the city's Chinatown.

Arnold Chung was loud in his claims of his family's aristocratic Chinese origins, and was determined to turn his clan into an aristocracy in British Guiana. Having seen how the Hakka Chinese prospered by growing their own produce, rearing their own livestock and running their own cookshops, groceries and laundries, he lost no time in getting his brothers to do the same, and by the end of the nineteenth century, two more of the brothers were on the way to prosperity.

One brother, James, opened a bakery where he employed Hakka, Portuguese and African women. The Portuguese women were excellent at making pastry and he sold their cakes as Chinese pastries, along with cakes made by the African women who had worked as servants for European women, who taught them to bake cakes adapted from English recipes, cakes then given such Creole names as salara, cassava pone, butterflap, cheese rolls, and tennis rolls. James Chung also began catering for the weddings and parties of the expatriate European community and the wealthy Georgetown middle class. Each Saturday, a long queue of Europeans and Creoles would form at his bakery, and by the end of the day everything would be sold out.

With the skills of his female employees at his disposal, he also organised them into sewing and knitting teams; later he opened a clothing factory and store where he sold bales of cloth, clothing, and sewing machines. In time he became so prosperous that he was able to send his eldest daughter, Elizabeth, to boarding school in England, with a plan for her to study medicine at Edinburgh University. She returned to become the first Chinese surgeon in the country.

But if the Georgetown Chungs were full of grand ambition, these passed Clarice's father by. Her mother belittled his lack of drive, telling him that he had lived too long on a sugar estate with Blacks and Indians, eating their creole food. Every Saturday, her mother insisted they took Clarice to a Chinese cookshop in Georgetown so she could eat Chinese food. She needed to eat food heavily seasoned with Shaosing rice wine, aniseed, cinnamon, and soya sauce to give her brains. They admired the achievements of her cousin, Joseph, who had gone to London to study law, and they put his cleverness down to the fact that his father had enough money to buy food from the Chinese cookshop and did not allow him to eat Creole food cooked by his Black and Indian servants. Chinese food would keep them Chinese, keep their aristocratic Chinese blood and brains pure, make them better than anyone else.

Clarice's father, George Chung, continued to run the carpentry section of the building business, working long hours away from home and returning drained and exhausted to his wooden cottage on Soesdyke estate. He was always complaining to his wife about their ill-treatment at his brother's hands, the low wages his brother paid him and his carpenters, cutting their pay when illness kept them from work, even his own pay, though his brother expected extreme loyalty from him.

Clarice loved her father deeply; he was the gentlest of the brothers, so loving and kind he felt more like a mother than a father. She felt the pain of his failure and saw how lonely he was when he sat silently in a corner for hours, deep in thought, sometimes with tears of shame in his eyes. Clarice felt her father's pain, but her mother, Sheila, did not. She would worsen it by complaining about the servant work she had to do for Arnold Chung, but blaming George for their poverty, and the fact that they had to live among poor Blacks and Indians.

So while Clarice's parents were ashamed to have to ask

Arnold Chung to help pay for the wedding, they had no choice.

To their surprise, Arnold agreed to to pay for Clarice's wedding, but he laid down his conditions. He wanted the wedding to be authentically Chinese, with all the rituals. He wanted it to be a public spectacle that would go down in history as the first true Chinese wedding in the colony, an event to which the prominent men in Georgetown could be invited. He would pay for everything, he would even travel to China himself to acquire everything needed to make it a truly Chinese wedding. He would return with ancestral tablets and materials for a shrine; he would pay for a traditional Chinese bridal costume for Clarice. Her parents were shocked by his generous offer but grateful. Perhaps, this was his way of compensating for paying George so poorly. It forced them, for a while, to revise their opinion of him and credit him with being kinder and more generous than they thought. They chastised themselves for thinking badly of him; they were prepared to forgive him his past misdeeds.

Arnold Chung did not do anything by halves. He contacted the editors of the two main newspapers in Georgetown to give them exclusive coverage of this historic event and soon news of the impending wedding of the niece of the prominent Chinese businessman Arnold Chung was on the front pages. One paper was given exclusive rights to take photographs and conduct interviews with Arnold, who would describe the symbolism and significance of the artefacts and rituals, starting with the ritual of matchmaking.

John's father and mother, William and Shirley Wong, were not happy about all this. They laughed uproariously when a piece appeared in the papers about the observance of matchmaking customs that preceded the engagement, which they knew was a lie. William had simply given John some money to buy Clarice a ring that looked like a diamond ring to mark their engagement. Meantime, Arnold Chung had asked the Chief Librarian at the public library to "research" material from an encyclopedia about traditional Chinese weddings and he sent these descriptions to the newspapers. The announcement of the engagement was accompanied by a sketch of a statue of the Chinese God of Matchmakers, Yue Lao, with a description of his role in the matchmaking ritual. The article said that John Wong and Clarice Chung had stood before a statue of Yue Lao while their feet were tied together with a strand of red thread and their parents lit joss sticks and prostrated themselves before the statue in the hope that the "old man" god would record their children's marriage in his "book of fate" and predestine its success. The piece claimed that the couple's horoscopes had been used to choose an auspicious date for the wedding. This was all lies; John's parents knew that Arnold was hijacking the wedding to garner prestige for himself; it was a political ploy, his way of gaining prominence among the leaders of Georgetown society. They nicknamed him *The Emperor*, but for the sake of their son's happiness and saving money they had to go along with it.

Clarice found herself having to visit Arnold Chung's house to have her wedding costume made by the seamstress he'd hired, whom he had personally instructed on its traditional design. Clarice did not like going to her uncle's house because their snobbery made her feel inferior and her cousins, Joseph and Jacob, enjoyed bullying her. Joseph would normally have been away studying law in England, but he and his sister, Elizabeth, had returned to British Guiana for their holidays. Clarice's mother said they were spoilt brats who ordered her about and made her wait on them, just like their father. She said that living in England had turned them into *gweilos*. They spoke like English

46

gweilos, ate only *gweilo* food and wore *gweilo* clothes. They rejected any Creole food set in front of them, and demanded that she wash and iron their clothes several times before they were satisfied. She would return home and weep with the shame of being treated like a servant by her husband's nieces and nephews.

Jacob, though, was mostly at home, tending the small zoo he had created in his father's garden. He had built a business hunting, killing and collecting rare animals, insects and birds to sell to European collectors who visited the colony to take back these creatures to embellish their collections. He would round up a team of men to take with him on his expeditions. With the help of Amerindian guides, they killed and skinned crocodiles and snakes to sell their skins to tourists. Jacob enjoyed associating with these people, and took to dressing like them, in a pith helmet, brandishing a walking stick and wearing thigh-high waders. He thought this made him look like a hunter. Sometimes he even carried an air rifle as he marched around the streets of Georgetown. The Wongs found him ridiculous and called him *Bwana* or *Bakra*. To cater for the tourists, Jacob also opened a shop that he named *The Interior*, where he also sold Amerindian artefacts – basketware, leather goods and food items such as casareep and cassava bread. He brought Amerindians to Georgetown to help in his shop, parading them as exotic objects to be gazed upon. The women demonstrated how they made cassava bread, and the men would paint themselves in dyes and wear colourful feather adornments for the amusement of the tourists – and locals, who gawped and pointed at them, calling them *Bucks*. As an extension of this business, Jacob opened a brothel in Tiger Bay where he employed some of the women as prostitutes and put the men to work in the rumshop.

Later, Jacob had discovered goldmining and persuaded his father to purchase a gold mine for him. They agreed to share the profits if Arnold would pay the Amerindian and Hakka men he employed to operate as diggers. This involved descending in cages into the pits to look for gold deposits, risking death in a muddy tomb. Arnold also encouraged Jacob to start a logging company to supply rare woods to the foreign market. For this, he secured contracts for Jacob and financed the purchase of jeeps, trucks, and chainsaws for felling trees.

At Arnold's house, Jacob kept cages for the monkeys, macaws, snakes, sloths, spiders, bats and birds he captured. Once, he lured Clarice into his zoo, locked her in an empty cage and kept her there long after darkness fell. In her terror she screamed for help but no one came to rescue her, though she was certain his parents and their servants could hear her screams. Later, her mother explained that Jacob was always locking up the servants in the zoo and tormenting them by releasing bats and spiders into the cages with them.

In the weeks before the wedding, Arnold and his wife held weekly rehearsals, attended by photographers from the papers, until everyone understood their parts and had perfected their performance of the rituals. There was a great deal of friction, especially over who should take some of the key roles. For example, a *Good Luck Woman* was required to dress the bride, then seat her in the sedan on which she would be carried to John's home, led, of course, by Arnold himself. This *Good Luck Woman* would have to bathe Clarice. The mother of the bride was not permitted to play this role, so Arnold's wife put herself forward. There were bitter quarrels when Clarice would not accept Auntie Margaret as her *Good Luck Woman*; she was not having someone she did not really know present at such an intimate occasion. Arnold thought that Clarice and her family should show their appreciation by letting his family play some of the important roles. The rituals also required the bride's younger brother to accompany her on her first visit to her parents as a married woman. Since Clarice did not have a younger brother, Arnold thought that Jacob should take the part, but she refused this idea vehemently, saying she did not want Jacob at her wedding at all, to which Arnold reacted, just as vehemently, saying he was sorry he had offered them any help at all. So many angry things were said, it was a wonder that they were still on speaking terms when the wedding day arrived.

On that day, small crowds of spectators, attracted by the newspaper descriptions of the rituals that would be enacted, gathered outside Clarice's home in Soesdyke, and outside the home of the Wongs in Georgetown.

The day before, the new wedding bed had been installed at the home of the Wongs; it was covered with symbols of fertility such as nuts, fruits and sweets, and children were required to sit on the bed and scramble for the sweets. The newspapers explained that the ritual was to make the couple's union fertile, so they would produce many children. They also explained that after the wedding ceremony, a rooster and hen would be hidden under the bed, and the first to emerge would indicate the gender of their first child. There were photos of the bed in the papers.

When it was time for Clarice to be bathed in the large tin tub, in water mixed with grapefruit juice, she could not bring herself to be naked even in the sight of her mother and locked herself away in her room. Normally, her aunt and uncle never visited them in Soesdyke, a place they hated to return to because it recalled their time there as sugar estate labourers, but on the wedding day, they were determined to oversee the enactment of all the rituals. Thus, they were present when Clarice locked herself away, and they called out to her, threatening to withdraw their help if she did not let Auntie Margaret play the role of the *Good Luck Woman* and bathe her. Clarice said she did not want any *Good Luck Woman*, she would bathe herself in the shower. Arnold told her it was not just a question of how she bathed, the *Good Luck Woman* would also say auspicious words as she bathed her; it was very important this was done, to bring her marriage good luck. Clarice did not care for any of these rituals. She thought it was all just superstition and she would have preferred a normal Christian wedding since it was far simpler, and cheaper, and they would not have needed his money.

At the Wong home, John was also throwing a tantrum. There, Arnold Chung had installed ancestral tablets. It was part of a capping ritual that John had to bow to his ancestors at the tablet while his father placed a cap of cypress leaves on his head, after which he had to bow to his parents. When it was time for him to put on the long red gown, red shoes and a sash with a silk ball on his shoulders, and do the bowing, John refused; he said he was not a slave or a servant to bow to anyone and he told the newspaper reporters and photographers to go away; this was a private wedding.

In Soesdyke, Clarice did not turn away the reporters so they were there to photograph her when she appeared resplendent in a red silk jacket, skirt and shoes, and the spectacular phoenix crown that held in place the red organza veil that hid her face. Tradition required the bride to be taken to the wedding ceremony on a red sedan. This Arnold had ruled out, offering instead to provide a car to take the bride to Georgetown, but her father, in a bid to win back some control of his daughter's wedding, insisted on providing a sedan that he made himself, based on his memory of wedding sedans he had seen in his boyhood in China. He improvised a tall wooden wheelchair with bicycle wheels, painted it red, upholstered it in red satin and embellished it with tassels and bells. He appeared with it proudly, with six of his carpentry apprentices who had offered to push it to Georgetown. When it appeared, the crowd applauded spontaneously, and though his brother scowled and told him he had built a donkey cart, George beamed with happiness as Clarice accepted his hand as he helped her into the sedan. He had given the small boys firecrackers to set off, and cymbals, bells and flutes to play, and so a traditional Chinese wedding procession made its way into Georgetown, followed by spectators who were happy to stop along the way and be treated to cold beer, soft drinks and Chinese cakes by Arnold Chung.

The next day, the papers were plastered with photos of the wedding procession in which Arnold Chung and his wife featured prominently.

When they arrived at William Wong's, he was waiting with the silk ball and sash from John's costume. This he had to place on the sedan chair after Clarice disembarked. The Wongs had also paid small boys to make as much noise as possible with squibs, bells and flutes. They had given out beers freely to the spectators, so they were drunk enough to jig along to the improvised music.

The bride's family were supposed to demand payment for handing over the bride. Clarice's parents did not like this part of the rituals and held back from performing it, but Arnold and his wife put on a show of good humour and giggling, demanding money before handing Clarice over to the Wongs. The crowd had read in the papers that this would happen and they joined in boisterously, shouting to William Wong, "Come on, Chineeman, hand over de money if you want the girl! Pay up, pay up!"

William gave a red envelope full of coins to Clarice's

parents, and she stepped onto the red mat they had laid out at the front door while her mother held a red parasol over her. She had to step over a small stove and have a pile of rice placed near her before John could raise the veil and look at her, then lead her to the new ancestral altar imported from Hong Kong. It was one of several Arnold had distributed to his brothers in an effort to bring back to them the tradition of ancestor-worship. He hoped it would catch on and the Chinese in the colony would thank him for returning their lost Chinese culture to them.

With Clarice beside him, John had recovered his temper and together they bowed to the ancestral altar and the statue of the kitchen god, Zao Jun, as they were required to do. This was followed by a tea-drinking ceremony when John's parents offered Clarice's parents a cup of tea with lotus seeds and dates. Finally, John and Clarice bowed to each other, shared a glass of wine and went to their bedroom to sit on their new bed and receive visitors. In spite of all the conflict it had caused, the wedding, the first authentic Chinese wedding in the colony, had left Clarice feeling intensely happy; it had made her feel very important.

★

All this had been a long time ago, when she was a pretty young woman. Now when people looked at her, bulky and impassive, they saw a strict, severe old Chinee lady, a widow, all alone, with no man to love and help her as John Wong had once done. John had died exhausted from overwork in Jacob Chung's gold mine in the interior. The Chungs had killed him, but she blamed herself for letting John have anything to do with them. If she had become hard and bitter, if that was what people thought of her, it was because her sufferings and struggles had made her tough; it was not her nature to be like that.

After the wedding, she had gone to live with John and his parents. How she loved that change in her life. They owned a two-storey house in Chinatown in Charlestown. On the ground floor were the grocery and bakery; they lived in the upper floor where there were three bedrooms, two bathrooms, a living room and a verandah. She learned to work in the grocery and bakery beside John and his parents. She loved serving the customers and her English improved because of having to communicate both in Creole and Standard English. At night the whole family would retire upstairs to rest, talk, and listen to music on the radio and gramophone. She learned to sing the English words of the songs – long forgotten – and to dance with John and his parents.

How happy she had been living with John and his parents, themselves happily married. In the bakery, she became very skilled at making cakes, and invented the *Chinee cake* that became so popular it always sold out. William Wong became the sole seller and distributed it all over the country. He made such a good profit and was so happy with Clarice, he began to pay her a salary, some of which she gave to her parents, the rest she put in a savings account. Earning her own salary gave her pride and confidence. Long after their wedding, John continued to behave as if they were courting. On Sundays he would take her for cycle rides around Georgetown, to look at the beautiful houses that John Sharples had built. They would dream about owning such a house one day, and she would tell John that she was saving up to do this. But it was not to be. She became pregnant, and just a few months before the birth of her first child, Norma, her father died, followed a month later by her mother. She scattered their ashes and bones into the Demerara river, at Stabroek, where they had disembarked from *The Admiral* in 1879, willing the waters to take them back to China where they belonged, where she too would return when she died.

For a time, living with the Wongs, Clarice continued to prosper. She bought a sewing machine and made clothes to sell in the shop. This increased her earnings, though a further pregnancy, that of Anna, followed. Then, in 1913, the whole of Chinatown burnt down and they became homeless. She had to beg her Uncle Arnold to rent them his bottom house in Kingston. This she regretted ever after, because that was when John met Jacob Chung.

She hated living with her uncle, and there was still her parent's cottage on Soesdyke estate, so she took them all to live there, using some of her savings to open a small shop. It barely earned enough money to keep them all – she, John, his parents, and their first two children, Norma and Anna. Anna was a sickly child, suffering frequent fits, making it difficult for Clarice to devote enough attention to the shop. It was after struggling for a few years in this way – meantime Frederick had been born – that John was prompted to take up the job that Jacob Chung offered him, managing the dredging works at his gold mine. Jacob also gave John shares in return for an investment, which Clarice made from her savings. John signed a contract with Jacob and went to work in the interior but the job made him very sick. He caught pneumonia and had to stay at home in Soesdyke, a dying man. Jacob and his brother Joseph visited them and made John sign over his investment and shares to them. After John died, Clarice found she was pregnant again. John's parents persuaded her to move to Berbice, because they were pining away for their old friends who, after the Charlestown fire, had all moved there, to the country's new Chinatown. This was how they came to move to Berbice, she and her three children, and John's parents. Together, they had opened the shop in Canefield, where Harold was born. Some time after, John's parents moved to the Corentyne and opened their own shop, leaving her alone with her four children.

★

Now, lying in her bed beside her newly married son and his wife, Clarice recalled her happiness on her wedding night. Now, here she was, an old Chinee lady who people thought was hard and bitter. They did not realise that she knew what it was like to be soft and young and pretty and in love. Frederick, she thought, looked just like his father, John Wong, when they were young and in love. She saw that he was brimming over with love for Mary Leo, just like his father used to be with her. Love made Frederick like a child. His eyes lit up when he looked at Mary. He could not bear not to be near her. He was always finding an excuse to touch her, and when he touched her, his eyes watered with love. He and Mary, in the bed next to hers, were trying to be quiet, but she heard the muted sounds of their lovemaking. She knew exactly what they were doing because she could remember very well what she and John Wong had done. The memory made her smile, and she lay there pretending to sleep, pretending she could not hear them. The memory was like good medicine for her. She could remember all the physical pleasure of her wedding night with John Wong. Her body was old and tired now, her skin was dry and wrinkled, but as the memory of the pleasures of her wedding night returned, for a moment her body felt young again, and she felt a fleeting second of sexual pleasure as she listened to the lovers in the next bed, as if they were she and John consummating their love for each other. It was a miracle that made her smile all night.

55

NEW DAY

In the morning, Lily and Mary woke to their first day of living on a sugar estate. At two in the morning, the noise of cooking began in the Indian logies, when the women rose to cook for the men who, an hour or two later, would file out to the roadside with pans of hot food slung on the pitchforks they carried across their shoulders. On their way out, they stopped at Clarice's shop to buy things to take to the canefields – cigarettes, matches, sweets, cakes and soft drinks.

While Lily learned to help Harold in the bakery, Mary helped Frederick in the shop. Frederick was always the first to open the doors and windows to greet the early customers. Mary learned to rise with him and begin the daily toil. First, they made the home-made drinks, then began the routine of serving the customers the small and cheap items they came for – an ounce of margarine wrapped in a small sheet of brown paper, a box of matches, a few ounces of salted cod or smoked herring, a nutmeg, a stick of cinnamon and other Indian spices, or a stick of cocoa, soft grease or a single bar of soap. The day was spent trudging the length of the shop to ferry these small items from the shelves to the customers, all for a few pennies only for each item. It left Mary nursing sore feet. Before they fell asleep, they rubbed their soles with Limacol astringent or Sacrool healing oil, but it brought little relief. The next day they had to resume the daily march up and down the shop. Those who could afford a weekly shop came at the end of the week

56

with a long list. Then, large bags of rice, flour, sugar and peas had to be lifted and weighed out on the scales. Not only their feet but the muscles of their arms and upper body were so sore they could barely move.

From her chair, Clarice watched Mary learn to become a Chinese shopkeeper. She learned by copying everything that Frederick did. She became his shadow, but she used her brain too, memorising the price of everything easily. Soon Mary did not need to be told what to do.

After a couple of months, Clarice, against her inclinations, found herself liking Mary, though she gave no clue to her feelings. She thought that Mary was growing close to her too, although at their first meeting, they had not liked each other. When Frederick was busy, Mary had to speak to Clarice and, gradually, they began to communicate more openly. Clarice would even leave her chair to show Mary how to weigh the Indian spices or smoked fish, or how to wrap the sticks of cocoa and soft grease.

With each passing week Mary's confidence grew until she became so efficient at working in the shop, she seemed to float effortlessly from one end to the other. Clarice and Frederick began to involve her in managing the accounts and stocktaking.

While Mary helped Frederick in the shop, Lily helped Harold in the bakery. It had been Norma's job to help there and in the shop, and she also supervised the servant girl in the kitchen, ensuring that she did the laundry and cleaned the kitchen, bedroom and yard properly. Clarice had liked Norma to supervise this work because she herself hated housework; she preferred to be in the shop. The shop was where money was made. Now, it seemed to Norma that Mary and Lily were replacing her in the household, so she began to spend more time in New Forest with Henry Singh and Doris. She usually took Anna with her, and this was a relief to Clarice, because Anna was only ever an intolerable burden.

However, with Norma staying in New Forest, Clarice no longer got the congee that Norma used to make for her breakfast, and she complained loudly and bitterly, and asked Mary and Lily to make it for her. They did not know what it was and told Clarice so. This sent Clarice into a rage, and she cursed and swore in Chinese and Creole.

Lily asked Frederick about congee.

He said, "Is porridge."

Lily told him that she would make porridge for Clarice in the morning and presented Clarice with a bowl of hot corn-meal porridge. When Clarice tasted the porridge, she spat it out, screamed and threw the bowl at Lily. It struck her on the head, covering her hair and face with the hot porridge. Lily howled in pain and recoiled in a corner, shaking in fear until Mary came to her rescue. She took her to the bathhouse where she bathed her, dried her and took her back to the kitchen, but Lily was in such shock she could not stop shaking, crying, and saying she wanted to go back to her home in Georgetown.

Mary said to Clarice, "I going to report this to the police. You can't do this to my sister. You coulda kill her. Lily not used to this kinda thing. Nobody never treat her bad. Lily don't treat nobody bad. I going to report you to the police."

Clarice picked up a cleaver, held it over Mary and Lily, and hissed, "You want report me to police? I going kill you first."

Harold took the cleaver from Clarice and pressed the sharp edge into her neck. "You want kill me wife? I going kill YOU first."

Frederick took the cleaver away from Harold, and said, "Mother, you can't treat we wife bad. You got to treat them good or else me and Harold going move out and build we own house and lef' you here alone. If you want we stay with you, you got to treat Mary and Lily good."

Lily asked them to send for her mother and sisters. Frederick went to the post office and sent a telegram to Susan Leo. She came two days later, with Jean and Sally. She said to Clarice, "Miss Chung, you can't treat my children like this. Lily don't deserve this, she is a quiet, gentle person. You nearly kill my chile. I don't want her live here if you don't treat her good. I prefer she come back home with me. I going take her home now."

Frederick had sent for Jimmy Chu who arrived in time to stop Susan taking Lily away.

Frederick said, "Mother, you did promise that Jimmy will build a house here in this yard for Harold and Lily to live, and for her mother and sisters to come and stay. Jimmy got to start building the house now now, and when it finish, Harold and Lily must live there." Frederick told Clarice that she must give Jimmy money to purchase building materials, and took her to the safe which she opened, then he took the money and gave it to Jimmy who said that he would not charge anything for building the house if his wedding with Sally could be held there as soon as it was finished; it could be a double wedding for Joe Persaud and Jean too. Clarice had to agree to this, or else both her sons would leave her.

Jimmy Chu built the two-storey house at the end of the yard, and when it was completed, Harold and Lily moved in. Then the double wedding was held for Jimmy and Sally, and Joe Persaud and Jean. Susan Leo did not have to pay anything for the wedding of her two daughters this time; she came as a guest and spent two weeks in the new house, long enough to see Sally settle down with Jimmy in a small cottage in the village of Dover just half a mile away. Jean moved in with Joe Persaud in a rented room in New

Amsterdam three miles away. Now, all her daughters were married and living with their husbands in Berbice, and Susan felt secure in the reassurances given to her by Frederick and Harold Wong that she was welcome to visit them anytime and stay in the new house, to see her daughters regularly.

There was now a little more room in the living space behind the shop, and when she was not working there, Mary spent more time in the kitchen where she prepared meals for herself and Frederick. Clarice noted how skilled Mary was at cooking African food. On Sundays, Mary cooked split-peas soup full of fufu, pig-tail, salted beef and dumplings. On Thursdays, she cooked *dry food* – boiled ground provisions eaten with salted cod in a sauce of fried onions, tomatoes and boiled eggs. Mary went to a lot of trouble to obtain a mortar and pestle for preparing the fufu. And just as she noted the pleasure that Mary took in cooking these dishes, Clarice also saw how easily she socialised with black customers in the shop. She remembered how Susan Leo had confessed to giving away Mary to be trained up for servant work by a black woman. One day she casually asked Mary if this was true, and then the story of Mary's life came out.

Mary told her yes, it was true, that when she was eight years old, her mother gave her away to live with Evadne Williams, a black woman, because she was not earning enough money as a laundress and market vendor to look after them all. Evadne bought fruit and grain from Susan's market stall, and Susan would tell her how hard it was to look after her daughters. So Evadne, who had worked as a maid in the homes of wealthy Chinese and white people in Georgetown, offered to take one of her daughters and train her to become a maid. Susan gave her Mary, and each week, Evadne would report to Susan that Mary was doing well, she was working hard, and not giving any trouble – only she often wet the bed. This last was true, but the greater truth was that from the first day that Mary went to live with her in rented rooms in the upper storey of a house in Charlestown, Evadne ill-treated her cruelly. As she instructed Mary how to cook, or wash and iron the laundry, she would physically and verbally abuse her. She slapped her and splashed her with hot water and hot oil. She put Mary to sleep on a mattress in the kitchen and her fear of Evadne was so great she often wet the mattress; then Evadne would tie a crapaud to her in a vain attempt to frighten her into controlling her bladder. When Evadne's boyfriend, a porter at the hospital, stayed with them, he would join in tormenting Mary. It was her job each morning to descend the back stairs and empty their bucket of urine over the roots of the fruit trees. Sometimes, they would follow her down the stairs and empty the bucket of urine over her.

Mary's sisters tried to rescue her. When Evadne was at work, they would visit her. She would weep and tell them about her ordeal and ask them to beg their mother to let her return home to Albuoystown, but Susan left her to continue her cruel four-year apprenticeship as a maid.

Clarice just nodded at the end of this tale, but she was smiling inwardly; it confirmed her view that this was all you could expect of black people.

Susan Leo had also given Lily and Sally to be fostered by Dr. Elizabeth Chung and her daughter-in-law, Elaine Li, but with them the girls received the best treatment possible, including an education at the convent school, and a high standard of living. Sally and Lily would sometimes take Mary to their foster homes where she could share a little of the good life that they enjoyed. It was shattering for Mary to see the difference. She admired the clothing in the two women's wardrobes and sat in the large cars parked outside their homes. Her sisters also took her to the department stores and banks where their foster parents took them. In the banks, Mary saw the smartly-dressed Chinese women who worked there. She admired their crisp white blouses and pencil-thin blue skirts and black, patent-leather shoes. She admired the way they strode around the bank, looking so elegant and efficient. She especially liked to look at the cashiers who sat in the cubicles with tills full of money. It made her long to grow up and become one of these beautiful, clever Chinese women in the bank, with their hands full of money. But she knew that without an education, with a mother who could not afford to raise her, such a dream was impossible.

Evadne Williams did not know about Mary's excursions to the homes of Elizabeth Chung and Elaine Li, or to see the clever, pretty Chinese girls in the bank, so she was constantly surprised about how Mary found the inspiration to keep on dreaming of a better life.

Only after she married Frederick Wong did Mary find herself in control of any money; it was not like the money in her dreams, but the dreams themselves did not die.

There were discouragements. When her mother-in-law told her about her royal Chinese heritage and her goal of passing it on to her descendants, she also made it clear that Mary was not one of the Chung clan, only a daughter-in-law, not related by blood, and not pure Chinese.

There was a cupboard in the kitchen where Clarice kept Chinese ingredients under lock and key that only Norma could use – five-spice powder, Shaoshing rice wine, black rice vinegar, sesame oil, *lapcheong* sausage, transparent rice noodles she called *funci*, soya sauce, *wanyi* fungus that Frederick called "rat ears", dried mushrooms, brittle yellow sticks of dried soya beans she called fuchuk. These were very expensive and available only in Georgetown so a taxi driver had to be hired to purchase them. The aroma from the cupboard was so strong you only had to stand near to smell it, but Clarice liked to open the door, stick her face right inside, take a deep breath and fill her lungs with the aromas.

On the last Sunday of the month, Norma would visit to cook a Chinese soup. All the dried vegetables would be boiled in their largest pot with a large slab of pork belly or a chicken. When the meat was cooked, it was drained and chopped into small pieces, and a dipping sauce made with salted garlic roasted in sesame oil, soya sauce and rice wine. Then Clarice and her children would sit round the table and eat noisily. Despite their husbands' protests, Mary and Lily were never invited to join them. Frederick and Harold would apologise to their wives but say it was best to humour the Old Lady. Mary and Lily could only look on, smelling the aroma of this food and hearing the noises of satisfaction the family made as they dipped morsels of meat into the sauce with one spoon, filled another spoon with soup and rice and slurped the contents of both spoons simultaneously into their mouths. It was a Chinese ritual for Chinese people.

LORNA

There was only one occasion when Mary felt any real acceptance from Clarice – when she gave birth to her first child, Lorna. All through her pregnancy, there was a buildup of expectation and suspense as to whether the baby would look Chinese or not. Clarice let it be known that if the baby *looked* Chinese, she would regard it *as* Chinese and therefore worthy of being welcomed into her illustrious clan and blessed with its gifts and talents. Everyone was in the yard waiting to see the baby, and there was huge relief when the midwife, after cleaning and wrapping her up, took her outside, held her up for viewing, and declared, "A real Chinee baby! She look just like her grandmother, Miss Clarice Chung!"

Clarice took the child, hugged her and declared, "Dis is a Chung baby! She going be a real Chung, with good brains, and very important, she going make plenty money!"

Mary was lying in bed exhausted, but she heard the blessing that Clarice gave her daughter, and she was glad for it, but then Norma came into the room, glared at Mary and said, "You daughter is not she first grandchild, is me daughter, Doris, who longtime she first grandchild and she mother is Chinee. Me! You ain't Chinee; you baby can't be Chinee; you baby is a coolie just like you!"

Clarice, who had followed Norma into the room, slapped her and said, "Shut you damn mouth! You shut you damn mouth. She child father is Chinee! You child father is

64

coolie!" This wounded Norma so much she sat on the landing and wept so uncontrollably that her brothers had to comfort her as she poured out her feelings. Mary heard every word.

Norma told her brothers that Mary had taken her place and pushed her out of their home. Their mother favoured Mary over her, treated her like her own daughter; now Mary was going to take over the shop, she was going to be the boss, and all her sisters, all the Leo women, were going to come and live in the new house. She complained that Clarice treated her like a servant, only wanting her to come and cook Chinese food, but she did not treat Mary like a servant, she treated her like the boss in the shop. She would not come and cook Chinese food for Clarice anymore; that would teach her a lesson.

Later, Frederick told his mother that she must do something to improve her relationship with Norma. Clarice admitted that as a young woman Norma had said she would never leave their house unless she married a man from Hong Kong, but at the time they could not afford the cost of paying a special Chinese matchmaker to arrange this, and then Norma had fallen pregnant for that coolie man. But she did feel sorry for Norma and wanted to make it up to her. She said that since Norma's daughter was now old enough to marry, she would try and find her a husband from Hong Kong. Thanks to Mary, the shop was doing well and there was enough money now to pay a matchmaker. Clarice asked Frederick to write Elizabeth Chung and ask her to arrange this.

At nights, Frederick and Mary liked to relax on the landing where they would sit and talk for hours. Even after their first child, they were still in love and enjoying their marriage. From her bed, Clarice liked to listen to their conversations. One night, she overheard Frederick telling Mary about his father, and trying to explain his mother's origins in China, so she got out of bed, sat at the open window where the moonlight shone on her face, and talked to them.

"When I come here from China with me family, dem people laugh an mock we. Dem Hakka Chinee 'pon deh boat, dem had pigtail. Me family, we was not Hakka Chinee, we was Punti; we had property we build in China and Hong Kong we used to rent; we was rich rich, we wasn't poor. We didn't come to B.G. because we ain't got money; British gov'ment send we to B.G. to help run the country. Dat is why dem help me Uncle Arnold get rich. Me family come from Chinee royal family. I going show you."

There was a trunk under her bed; Clarice opened it and took out a yellowing scroll. She gave Frederick a torchlight and told him to shine it on the scroll and let Mary look at it good.

"You see dis picture here? Dis me ancestor, he name Emperor Chengzong. You see what he wearing? Dat is he yellow dragon coat. Me whole clan, Chung clan, all a we work fo' this emperor. From ahwe, he get plenty soldier and civil servant, an we look after he. He give we castle to live in, land to farm and plant, in a place name Heilongiiang. Look, me Uncle Arnold write down de name 'pon dis piece a paper. We mind sheep, we grow rice, greens and fruit, and we used to give the emperor everything we grow on his land. We bake fo' he and he family, we give them meat and milk. We was his own people an' he treat we good good; he say we is he own family; he give we this scroll with he picture, an we bring it pon de boat to B.G."

When she finished, she told Frederick to roll up the scroll and she replaced it in the trunk. Then she showed Mary three silk pouches that her family brought with them from China. One pouch was full of old silver coins, the other two contained seeds. Clarice explained that one set of seeds were soya beans, the other the seeds of the plum tree that grew near their house in Hong Kong. It was a beautiful tree, it produced the most beautiful flowers. When they left China, her mother cried because she would never see those beautiful plum trees again; when they lived on Soesdyke estate, they planted those seeds but they never grew. Clarice said that nothing from China could grow good in British Guiana, not even people; this country was no good for Chinee people, it was a bad place for them. She concluded gloomily that only when she died and went to heaven and met her ancestors, then she would plant the seeds there, with help from God and they would grow. They had to put everything in her coffin when she died, including the scroll, the silver coins and seeds.

"You ain't going dead yet, Mother," Frederick said. "You got long to live."

She grunted, "I going dead, yes. I want dead, because I don' want live in dis kiss-me-ass country no more. I want dead because is only then I goin' leave dis country. I want dead, yes."

Mary also tried to reassure her. "No, Mother Chung, don't say so. What about you gran'chilren? You don' want to live to see all you gran'chilren?"

"No," she replied, "you can't give me Chinee gran'chilren. I want Chinee gran'chilren. You ain't Chinee, you is half coolie, so you children can't be Chinee, never! When I come here, I had was to stop bein' a Chinee. I had to stop talkin' like a Chinee, we had was to stop eatin' Chinee food, we had was to start eatin' black and coolie food. We ain't Chinee no more if we live in this country. Look at you mother; she ain't no Chinee, she turn coolie. If you get more pickney, they going turn coolie too, because dis is a coolie place we livin' in. Coolie an' black. It ain't no

67

good fo' Chinee people. I sorry I ever come to dis country. I want dead an' go 'long me way an' never see dis country again. It can only turn we Chinee people into coolie an black people."

Mary said, "Oh Lord, Mother Chung, don' say so. Chinee people do good in dis country, like your uncle Arnold and he pickney. Look how you own cousin is doctor an' lawyer and got gold mine. No, man, Chinee people do good in dis country. Look, in Georgetown, if you go in dem bank, it full a beautiful Chinee girl workin'. When I was small girl, I use to go in dem bank an watch dem Chinee girl. I did want to grow up and work in the bank like dem. I hear dem bank manager prefer to hire dem Chinee girl; dey trus' Chinee people. In Georgetown, Chinee people do good. Dem is de best doctor, dentist and business people, best people in dis country."

Clarice snapped, "In Georgetown, yes, but not here in dis kiss-me-ass estate! Look where I end up, 'pon sugar estate! All me life in dis country I had to live pon sugar estate. I try and try not to end up pon a blasted sugar estate, but I still end up here."

Mary said, "But you do good, Mother Chung; you husband dead an' lef' you, yes, but look how by you'self, you alone manage to get you own shop an' make money an' mind you own chil'ren. My mother din' do good like you."

Mary's voice broke because it pained her to compare her own mother's failures to Clarice's success, and Clarice noticed this. She hadn't given away her own children because she was too poor to mind them, and it was obvious to her that Mary had fared the worst, having to live with a black woman who ill-treated her, while two of her sisters had lived in luxury with a wealthy Chinese family. She saw how Mary put up a brave front and acted like she was stronger than she really was. Mary tried to bluff her way through life, but she could see straight through her. It made Clarice feel good to see Mary's weakness; it meant that she could prevent Mary from taking advantage of her.

Clarice said, "Life ain't easy, life hard hard hard, but you got to bear it, you got to be strong and bear it. Me life was hard hard hard. Don' t'ink is only *you* life hard when you was a chile. Me life was harder dan you life. Me Chinee name was Cheung Tse; dat is de Chinee name I come to B.G. with. If you had was to leave China like me on dat stinking boat we come in, you woulda dead, but I din' dead because I was a strong strong Chinee pickney. Dat is why I din' dead; is me royal Chinee blood mek me strong. Dem keep we like pig in dat boat; it name *Admiral*. Was me and me whole family; dem put we in dat boat wit' two hundred Hakka people. All a we live in de middle inside dat boat. Dey keep we like pig, stink stink stink. Dem feed we salt beef, salt fish an' biscuit, an' only water fo drink, no tea. Dem give we bucket fo' pee an' shit in, an' dem Hakka people din use no bucket, dem pee an' shit all over. Is a good ting dey use to put sawdust to cover up dem shit an' pee, but it still stink. Oh gawd, night an' day dat ship stink. Dem had a lil bathroom an toilet upstairs dem 'low me mother, me an' me auntie to use, so me mother an' auntie an' me we use to go upstairs to bathe an' use toilet sometimes, but Gawd, dat boat always rockin' an' we couldn't stand up, we use to fall down an' dem white sailor dem always watching me mother and me auntie to see dem naked. I tell you, you tink you had hard life? We had hard hard life on dat boat. Sometimes my mother say she want jump in de water an' dead, she would prefer to dead than stay on dat stinkin', nasty boat. I ain't know how all a we din' dead. Dem Hakka people did hate we. When we tell dem Emperor Chengzong was we ancestor, dem say he ain't no Chinee, he is Mongol barbarian dat does eat horsemeat raw, an' drink blood, an'

Mongol people ain't Chinee, how Hakka people start Taiping revolution to kill out Mongol people. Dem tell me I look like Mongol, not Chinee, an they going kill we whole family. Every day they threaten to kill we, an' dey fight plenty wid me father an he three brother. I did frighten bad. Three month we live like dat! Three month! Den when we reach B.G., dey put we to live 'pon Soesdyke estate. Oh Gawd, dat place was terrible, worse dan dat boat. All a we had to live in a small small cottage, with no furniture, nothing, an' we had to live with dem poor poor black an' coolie people, use same latrine like dem, an all a we had was to work in the canefield an cut an burn cane an' weed canal an' clean punt. An dem hardly pay we any money. Was a hard hard life. We suffer bad. We was never so poor, never! We had was to eat coolie and black people food. We get sick, all a we. Is lucky me father-in-law, William Wong, he had shop in Georgetown. He hear how we punishin' and he bring furniture an' stove an' he give we food an tell we to pay back later, when we get money. He an' my father turn friend; dat is how come I meet Frederick father, John Wong, an' we married. You tink you had hard life because you mother give you 'way to black people? Well, me mother give me 'way to black lady to mind, too. Dat lady name was Clarice Johnson, dat is how I get dat name: Clarice; she give me she name. She was servant fo' white overseer; dey give she nice cottage an' give she dem book an magazine, too. Clarice used to go to church an' learn to read an' write; she had education, an she give me lil education; she teach me English, an' to read an' write lil bit; she help me and give me she name. I learn to eat an' cook her food, make metagee and fufu soup. So don' tink you suffer more dan me, Mary, you ain't suffer more dan me."

Frederick could see that Clarice was upsetting Mary so he told her to stop talking about bad things to his wife, and only speak to her about good things; he did not want to hear any more about her suffering, he was not interested, and he blew out the light in the paraffin lamp and took Mary to sleep on the rice sacks in the shop that night, angry with his mother. He did not like it when his mother described her life as a bad one. He was proud of her because she came from China, she was a genuine Chinese, she could still speak some Chinese words, her history in China was a great one, her family were linked to a Chinese emperor, they even owned a scroll picture of him that he had given to them. Her Uncle Arnold had written down the name of the place in China they came from and he wished he could go there and visit their ancestral home. He liked to tell people about it; it made him feel like a real Chinese, but his mother spoiled it by portraying her life differently, as one of suffering. Here in Canefield, there was only poverty and the hard life of the Indian workers on the sugar estate, but his mother had lived in China, the greatest, most ancient culture on earth, but she spoiled it and let him down when she told Mary she had to live like a pig on a stinking ship for three months. He told Mary not to believe what she said; it was not true; she and her family were actually treated very well on their journey to British Guiana. They came on the last ship to bring Chinese people to British Guiana, in 1879; they did not come to British Guiana to work on the sugar estates, they came here as Christian missionaries, and because the Cheung brothers were also builders in Hong Kong, that is why they were sent to British Guiana, to build churches, and spread Christianity among the Hakka Chinese. He told Mary the reason why the Chung family were so successful in Georgetown was because of the privileges they received from the British government in return for their services to them in Hong Kong. The success of his mother's family in Georgetown was proof of their aristocratic origins in China; his mother was forgetting this because she was getting old.

Mary felt puzzled, and told him she did not know which version of Clarice's origins to believe. He told her to believe his version; it was the version she used to tell him when he was a little boy, but now that she was getting old, her brain was not so good, and she was forgetting her real history. Mary agreed with him, and said she would not listen to Clarice again when she made her life sound worse than it was. Frederick told her that in the trunk under the bed was a small notebook in which Arnold Chung had written down notes about their origins in China. In it he had described where they lived in Hong Kong, had written down the names of the churches they built, had written down the name of Hong Kong in the Mandarin language they spoke when they came to British Guiana. He used to call it *Xian Gang*. It proved that they were not Hakka Chinese. When they came to British Guiana, his mother used to speak a little Mandarin. He told Mary that sometimes in her sleep, when she was dreaming about China, he would hear her speaking Mandarin, but no more; she was getting old and talking about dying, because she was forgetting who she really was. He was worried about this, he was worried that Clarice was losing her sanity, like his sister Anna. He was worried Clarice was becoming insane in her old age.

Frederick need not have worried about Clarice's state of mind because Dr. Elizabeth Chung wrote to give her news that gave her a new lease of life. The Chinese matchmaker had found a Hong Kong husband for Doris and he would be bringing him to Canefield to make the match. This news made Clarice and Norma very happy.

After a week, the matchmaker came with Mr. Feng Chow and his son Willy. Clarice received them in the shop and served them chilled drinks and cakes. Feng Chow did not speak any English, nor did Willy, so the matchmaker had to translate between them. Clarice told Feng Chow that she came from China a long time ago; she wanted him to know she was a pure Chinese person, a Punti with a royal ancestor, descended from Emperor Chengzong. She explained how they came to travel to British Guiana through a sense of obligation to the Christian missionaries, who they repaid by promising to build churches in British Guiana and convert the Hakkas to Christianity; she wanted him to know that her family had fled China to escape the Hakka Taiping rebellion.

Mr. Chow frowned at this but Clarice did not notice. He had assumed that Clarice spoke his language so, at first, he spoke to her in Cantonese, and Clarice smiled and nodded as if she understood. When it dawned on Mr. Chow that she did not speak his language and that she disapproved of Hakka people, he asked the translator to tell her that he was a Hakka, and so was his son. Further, he was a proud Hakka man; his ancestors had been part of the Taiping rebellion, they wanted to rid China of emperors.

Clarice, though, still wanted to make a match for Doris, and told Mr. Chow she was happy with him and his son being Hakka. She signalled Doris to come forward to meet and shake hands with Willy. When she was asked if she liked Willy, she nodded. Then Mr. Chow told Clarice that he expected her to provide Willy with a shop of his own. In Hong Kong, he owned his own shop which Willy ran. He was willing to help pay for the shop. Clarice agreed – Jimmy Chu would build the shop for them – and a wedding date was set. Mr. Chow insisted that the shop must be ready in time for the wedding, and above the shop there should be four bedrooms since he, his friends and family intended to come and stay with Willy sometimes. He had come with money and he gave this to Clarice to help with building the shop.

In a few months, the shop was built in New Forest. As soon as they received news that it was completed, Willy Chow's family set off from Hong Kong. This time they came with a couple of young men, Willy's friends. They picked up a car in Georgetown and spent the first few days racing up and down the dirt roads. They were curious about the forest in Dover and told Clarice they would go there to find food for themselves; she would not need to provide them with goods from her shop. They told her they liked to eat wild meat. They caught a giant turtle, a young tapir and baby alligator and brought these creatures, still alive, back to Clarice's shop where they let them loose. When they untied these creatures, Norma was there with Doris and Anna. All the women screamed in terror when the tapir began to run around the shop and the alligator slithered around, snapping its jaws. The Chinese men attacked the animals with axes, cutlasses and cleavers. Frederick and Harold had to help them take the dead creatures into the yard where they skinned the tapir and chopped it into pieces. It was more difficult to kill the turtle and chop it up. The turtle resisted all their efforts to break its shell. For a long time, it lay on its back with its underbelly heaving.

The scene of slaughter disturbed Anna who was gripped by a fit and fell to the ground, foaming at the mouth. Mary and Lily looked on in horror; they had never got used to how Clarice and her family dealt with Anna's fits. Clarice and Norma grabbed a bucket of water each and doused her, as if they were putting out a fire. The soaking did nothing to pacify Anna; it only prolonged her fit. Then Harold, Frederick and Norma did what their mother had taught them to do. They brought out ropes and tied her securely, then took her to the latrine where they locked her in. She screamed all the time she was locked in the latrine. Later, they took her to the bedroom and tied her to the bed. The men from Hong Kong were convinced that Anna was insane, and there was insanity in this family. They advised Mr. Chow not to proceed with the wedding or else Doris was going to give him insane grandchildren. Mr. Chow used sign language to tell Clarice he did not want the wedding to proceed because of the insanity in her family. Clarice shook her head and hands vigorously by way of denying his charge, then she went to her safe, took out money, and started to give it all to Mr. Chow. This pacified him.

Meantime, Anna had freed herself from the ropes and run away. The visitors ignored this and resumed turning the turtle into soup and spit-roasting the tapir and alligator in the yard. In spite of the horror that had accompanied the preparations, all were impressed by their cooking skills.

75

They had brought their own spices, ginger, fungi, Chinese sausages, rice vinegars and other ingredients from Hong Kong, and had even brought their own chopsticks and bowls. They served turtle soup, barbecued pork and egg fried rice to Clarice and her family, who were all intoxicated by the delicious tastes and ate heartily, feeling privileged to be eating such authentic Chinese food.

They had long finished eating when Clarice told Harold and Frederick to go to the forest in New Forest to look for Anna. It was where she always went when she ran away. She liked to sit by the river and look at the water because it had a calming effect on her, but they had left it too late. When they got to Dover, Henry Singh told them that Anna had taken the bus to the ferry; she had asked him for money and told him she was going to Georgetown to see Dr. Chung to beg her to make her better. The bus driver confirmed he had taken Anna to the ferry where she was planning to cross the river and get a train to Georgetown. Frederick went to the post office to send a message to Elizabeth Chung, to tell her that Anna was coming to see her and she must send her home at once in one of the taxis that ferried people to and from Berbice.

But later that day, Clarice received a telegram from Elizabeth reporting that Anna had reached Georgetown, but had gone to the seawall where she walked into the ocean and drowned herself. She had visited Elizabeth to tell her she was going to kill herself in the ocean because her mother always said that if their corpses were thrown into the ocean, their bones would find their way back to China and their ancestors. Then Anna had run away before anyone could stop her. Clarice asked Elizabeth to arrange Anna's cremation, and scatter her ashes in the Demerara River, near Stabroek, where she had disembarked with her family in 1879. She would pray for Anna to find her way back to China to their royal ancestors.

For the day of Doris's and Willy's wedding, the young men from Hong Kong went to hunt for more wild meat. Whilst they were away, Willy's father did not speak to anyone, but sat in a corner of the shop, near the money drawer, with a stack of Hong Kong newspapers and read them one by one, raising them high enough to conceal his face from view.

The young men captured another turtle, tapir and baby crocodile. Back at the yard, they danced around the creatures, prodding them for the entertainment of the guests. They especially enjoyed tormenting the turtle by turning it on its back, spinning it around and watching it wave its legs frantically in the air. It made them laugh until they cried. But not even this distracted Willy's father from reading his newspapers. Another meal of turtle soup, barbecued tapir and crocodile with egg fried rice was spread out on a large table. Only then did Feng Chow fold away his newspapers, but he did not sit at the table to eat with everyone. He took a bowl of food back to his chair in the shop, and sat there eating contentedly with chopsticks. Clarice and Mrs. Chow smiled and nodded at each other.

The registrar from the town hall in New Amsterdam came to officiate. Doris wore a red dress and a broad-brimmed hat covered with a red organza veil. When she appeared, Clarice and Norma clapped in excitement, but Doris was so terrified she shook with nerves.

Afterwards, Frederick told Norma he was worried that Doris and Willy would not be able to communicate, but she pointed out that Willy was trying very hard to learn some English, and she felt certain that he and Doris would be able to talk to each other well enough to have a happy marriage.

She said that Willy would look after Doris and they would give her real Chinese grandchildren. Clarice, impatient with this discussion, said she was very happy because her dream had come true – Doris's marriage had brought a real Chinese person into her family. She could die in peace knowing that Doris would have pure Chinese children who, by virtue of their pure Chinese blood and culture, would be rich and successful people. She hoped that on their wedding night, Doris would conceive a pure Chinese child, and though she would not live to see it grow, from the other side she would watch over it and ensure its success in the world.

If Frederick saw the contradictions in what his mother regarded as "pure", he said nothing.

That night, Clarice felt exhausted, but sat talking on the landing with her sons and their wives because she felt full of feelings that were hard to express. She looked at Frederick and Mary. She could see that he loved her, liked to be near her and touch her. Clarice remembered again how much she loved John Wong when they married. That night, she was full of that old feeling of love, but she felt pain, too, the pain of grief. Both feelings were storming in her so much, she could not speak. The words she wanted to say stuck in her throat, but in her silence she thought about Doris, and felt sad that she was not in love with Willy Chow, though she was lying in a bed with him. She sighed and said she was going to bed.

To their surprise, Clarice's sons and daughters in-law heard Clarice singing. Frederick recognised it as a lullaby she used to sing to him when he was a very small boy. She said it was a song that her mother used to sing to her when she was a baby in China. When they were on the boat to British Guiana, though she, Clarice, was distressed and could not sleep, her mother had felt too sad to sing the song to her and once they were in British Guiana, she forgot the words, but Clarice said that she would never forget it. Frederick realised that Clarice had kept this song in her heart through all her life, and now she was singing it to herself, gently and sweetly, in Chinese:

> The moon is bright, the wind is quiet,
> The tree leaves hang over the window,
> My little baby, go to sleep quickly,
> Sleep, dream sweet dreams.

In the morning, Clarice did not rise early as she usually did, so Frederick went to wake her, but could not rouse her. They put out the white flag, a signal for the doctor to stop at the shop on his daily rounds but, impatient with waiting, Harold took the bus into New Amsterdam and called on the doctor, who drove back with him to Canefield. The doctor examined Clarice's body and declared that she had died of a heart attack in her sleep. He sat on the landing with Clarice's sons, their wives and Norma, who was wailing and weeping. He told them it was Clarice's diabetes that had killed her; perhaps she had overeaten at Doris's wedding, eaten too much rice. It might have given her a huge glucose spike. He had warned her to stop eating so much of Norma's rice congee in the morning; it was bad for her, but she liked her Chinese food too much. Norma felt that the doctor was blaming her for Clarice's death and declared, "If I din' cook congee fo' she, she woulda starve to death. Dem (she pointed to Mary) can only cook black an coolie people food like dhal, an' plantain fufu an split peas soup."

The doctor said, "Dhal would have been better for her than rice congee, dhal was the right food, and the split pea soup too. I told your mother to eat what her daughter-in-law was cooking for her, but your mother was a difficult

79

patient, she thought she knew better than me." He turned to Mary and reassured her that she had done her best for Clarice, and not to take the blame for her death, but after he left, Norma continued to blame Mary, saying that it was her creole cooking that had killed her mother.

Clarice's funeral was held on a very rainy day. Her cousin, Elizabeth Chung, did not come for the funeral because she was too busy in Georgetown. Frederick, Harold and Norma wept copiously over Clarice's corpse, but they were so heavy-hearted and distracted by grief that they forgot Clarice's instructions to place the Chinese heirlooms in her coffin. Only when her coffin was placed in the grave, which was full of water from the heavy rain, did Frederick remember that they had forgotten to place her heirlooms in it, but he reasoned that this was just as well since her coffin would be full of water, and this would have destroyed the scroll painting of the Emperor, so it would be no use to Clarice when she got to heaven. She had always said she needed that scroll picture in her coffin so that, in heaven, she would recognise her imperial ancestor. Frederick was sure that Clarice would recognise him from memory. Harold disagreed, saying that it was so long ago since Clarice left China, she could not remember anything about it; she had told him so.

AFTER CLARICE

After Clarice's death, her children agreed that Frederick and Mary should run the shop, take an income from it and continue to live there with their children in one corner of the yard, while Harold and Lily would live in the two-storeyed house in the opposite corner where they would manage the bakery and take the income it earned. Norma decided that she would leave Canefield and live permanently in New Forest so she could be near her daughter and help in the Chow shop alongside Willy, his father and Doris. The shop in Canefield reminded her too much of her dead mother and she could not bear to go there and see that the money drawer was now guarded by Mary. She went to the shop only when she wanted to see her favourite brother, Frederick. He was fond of Chinese roast duck, so each time Willy cooked one, she wrapped some in greaseproof paper and brought it to him. She would lean on the counter to speak to him while ignoring Mary.

This reminded Mary of when Norma made Chinese soup and she was never offered any. It brought back the pain that Clarice so often caused her. Clarice was dead but Norma enjoyed reminding Mary that her mother had never accepted her. It was easy to hurt Mary.

When she came, Norma noticed the changes Mary had made in the shop. The shelves now displayed tinned foodstuffs introduced to attract a better class of customers than the poor people who lived in the logies, foods that the

European overseers liked to eat – tinned corned beef, hams, fish and fruits – as well as patent medicines, including various brands of aspirins, antiseptic cream, plasters and cough mixtures. These days, the servants of the white overseers made a point of shopping there, because Mary liked to talk to them about their employers, and the servants enjoyed telling her about their habits. Norma remarked that the home-made ointment Clarice used to make was all the medicine the customers in the logies ever needed. It rankled that Mary had become so ambitious and confident as a shopkeeper, skills passed on to her by Clarice, but she realised that she could not compete with her. The overseers lived in Canefield near the shop and it was easy for their servants to walk there. Willy's shop in Dover was too far from the plantation for Norma to do what Mary was doing. However, when she overheard some customers asking Frederick for Clarice's ointment, it gave her the idea of making this salve and selling it in the Chow shop – and this drew the estate workers from Canefield all the way to Dover to buy it. As she grew older, Norma resembled her mother more and more, and although, Clarice had not treated the people from the logies well, she had become such a fixture in their lives that her death left a gap, and when they went to Willy's shop, it was as much to be reminded of Clarice by Norma as to buy the home-made ointment she sold. It was not only this they went for, but also the "Chinee cake" and malted milk drink that Clarice used to make, which Norma now made.

Norma was quick to boast that people from the logies were walking all the way to New Forest just to buy these things. None of this bothered Mary; she had no wish to compete; the estate workers' custom did not bring in enough profit. Clarice had once tried to teach Mary how to make "Chinee cake", but her lessons were always accompanied by cruel comments about Mary's lack of real Chinese blood – the reason why she couldn't learn to cook Chinese food. It was in part to erase Clarice's influence that Mary sought to put her own stamp on the shop, and raise its standards. Even so she did not like it when Norma boasted that Willy's shop was doing so well that his father had offered to build her a shop next door, where she and Henry Singh could live near Doris, who was expecting her first child. Worse, when the new shop was built, Mary noticed that some of her old customers no longer came to her, but travelled to New Forest to shop for their weekly groceries. Some of them even came to tell her that Norma was giving them special discounts if they shopped with her. This was competition.

Mary's second child, Joan, was born in the shop, but she came too late to receive the good luck blessings from Clarice that Lorna had received. It was, perhaps, just as well; Mary thought that Joan did not look as Chinese as Lorna and knew that this would not have pleased Clarice; she imagined the silent displeasure that might have greeted this birth. Whenever she looked at Joan, she was reminded of Clarice's constant displeasure with her that she was not pure Chinese. It did not help that when Doris's first child, Evelyn, was born, Norma came to tell Mary that not only did she look totally Chinese, she would grow up a real Chinese in the culture provided by Willy and his family. They would teach her to speak Chinese and take her to Hong Kong. She said that she was certain that Clarice was looking down from heaven, minding the interests of her first really Chinese grandchild. Thus did Clarice Chung continue to live like a ghost in the minds of the family she had left behind.

GENIUS

When Lorna was five years old, she was sent to St. Peter's school where, after only a month, the headmaster, Mr. Wellington, excitedly pronounced her a mathematical genius. He visited Mary and Frederick to discuss Lorna's future. He told them that he would personally supervise Lorna's education and coach her to win a scholarship to attend the best girls' school in Georgetown, St. Rose's High School. Perhaps Lorna might then win a scholarship to go to university in England, where she could study to become anything she wanted to be – a doctor or lawyer, anything.

Mary was so overwhelmed by feelings of pleasure and gratitude that she wept for two days and thought her heart would burst. She was so distracted by dreams about what the future might bring, thanks to Lorna's genius, she could not concentrate on her work. She told all her customers about it, told them that Mr. Wellington had said that Lorna would go to England to study. The news spread in Canefield and Lorna became quite a celebrity. People remembered that Clarice Chung used to say that her family's blood was royal Chinese blood, and they concluded that it was this that made Lorna a genius. Naturally, they wondered if Clarice's other great grandchild, Evelyn Chow, was also a genius. Norma enrolled Evelyn in Mr. Wellington's class, and waited to see if he would pronounce Evelyn a prodigy like Lorna, but he did not. This disappointed Norma who feared that Mary would lord it over her, but Mary was careful not to discuss Lorna's education when Norma visited them, even though Lorna had become her greatest pride and joy. In the reflected glory of Lorna's genius, Mary found an antidote to the pains she had suffered. Lorna gave substance to her dreams.

Mary gave birth to two more children, Andrew and Phillip. By now, their cottage had become too small for them. Luckily, the big company, Bookers, who owned this estate and many others, decided to demolish the logies, and were offering the chance of new housing to everyone in Canefield, including Frederick and his family. They would lease people land, and offer a loan to help them build new houses. Harold and Lily decided not to take up this offer; they would leave Canefield and move to Georgetown and open their own shop there.

Mary did not want to return to Georgetown. She had done well in Canefield with Frederick, and Lorna was doing well at school, under Mr. Wellington's supervision. They would stay and build a larger home, with a bigger shop and kitchen on the ground floor, with three bed-rooms, a bathroom and a living room on the upper floor. Her mother and her sisters, Jean and Sally, liked to visit. Her sisters had growing children of their own, so with a bigger house she could accommodate them when they came. As a child, she'd had to leave her family home because her mother could not afford to keep her; now she was in a position to house them all; she was proud of this great improvement in her life. By her own efforts she had freed herself from deprivation and despair; she was in control of her own life, she was secure. She had a good husband who loved her and was happy to share everything he had with her.

This should have erased all the pain she had felt in her life, but it was not to be. While the house was being built, she received an anonymous letter warning her not to move into the new home or else bad luck would strike her family. It unnerved her to think that someone might be jealous enough to work obeah on them, so when the house was completed, and before they moved in, she inspected it for evidence of hidden obeah paraphernalia. She found three small parcels wrapped in black cloth and tied with string. In them were random objects – chicken feathers and the large teeth of an animal. She threw the parcels away in the canal, and told herself to forget about them, not to let them prey on her mind. She threw the letter into the latrine, and the family moved into their new home, but it bothered her that she did not know who had sent the letter.

Even in moments of pleasure, feelings of anxiety haunted her. It was a shadow she did not have the strength to banish. When she had first come to live in Berbice, her mother-in-law had made her feel worthless. Now that woman's daughter had replaced her in having that power, and it occurred to her that it might be Norma who had sent the letter; she was the only person who bore her such malice.

In the new house, there were so many decisions to make about organising the shop and so much unpacking to do that there should have been no time to dwell on these anxieties. But it did not seem real that this beautiful house belonged to her.

It wasn't that she couldn't think realistically about her position. For instance, across the road was the home of the Yusufs, who owned the cinema. It was a house she had always envied. It was the largest, finest house owned by a Black or Indian person in Canefield; it was full of modern conveniences. Mrs. Yusuf's servant, Bibi, who was a regular customer in the shop, had told her everything about the house – that the bathroom was tiled wall to wall – even the floor; that the kitchen, too, was tiled, and all the work surfaces were covered in arborite laminated panels and that Mrs. Yusuf owned the latest pyrex ovenware. Her new house was not as luxurious as Mrs. Yusuf's; she had not acquired the things that Mrs. Yusuf had and this might have tempted her to feel inferior. But she told herself not to compare her home in a bad way with Mrs. Yusuf's – the cinema brought in a bigger income than her shop ever could, and this is why she could not compete with her, so she busied herself with settling into her new home.

The house still smelled of new paint, reminding her that it was the start of a new life, that her life had changed, but only one thing, one person, reassured her that her life had really changed for the better: Lorna. Lorna had become the light that could banish the darkness inside her. Lorna would go away to study in England and return to a high status profession, earning a lot of money. She would own a large property, she would be able to look after her parents and they would share in her wealth and status. Lorna would free her from her past.

She gave Lorna a position of privilege among her children. When she served them meals, Lorna was given the largest helpings, the best cuts of meat. Lorna was given vitamin supplements to take with her meals, to strengthen her resistance to illness because she was prone to colds and flu – she was a delicate child because her brain worked so hard. And though Mary did not consciously intend it, whilst Lorna was favoured, she turned her other daughter, Joan, into a servant.

In the larger house there was more housework to be done, more floor to sweep and polish, more laundry to do with the extra bed linen: these were the jobs that Mary assigned to Joan. For although, in her own way, she was a good pupil at school, Joan was not a genius; there was no illustrious academic future mapped out for her, and the headmaster and his teachers gave her no special attention. But what Joan had was an instinctive and passionate love of reading and writing. From the age of six, she began to visit the small library at the sugar estate community centre with Lorna, and would borrow three books a week. She would take these books home, read and return them, then borrow another three. She developed excellent skills in spelling, comprehension and essay-writing, but the headmaster was unshakeable in his determination to see Lorna as the superior student in every way. Once, when he visited the shop, Frederick asked him for his assessment of Joan's abilities. Mr. Wellington shook his head vigorously. While Joan was a keen reader who was accomplished in English, she was poor at mathematics, and was therefore incapable of winning a scholarship that would pay for her secondary education. Unless her parents could afford to pay for her, she would not have one like her gifted sister. He shook his head and said that Joan would be better off learning to be a shopkeeper like her mother.

All this reinforced the way Mary treated Joan. She told Frederick that they could not afford to send Joan to secondary school; the education of her two brothers had to be given priority. So, Mary began to teach Joan to do the housework in exactly the way that Evadne Williams had taught her, gave her the same jobs. In the mornings, Joan had to empty the urine bucket used by the whole family. As soon as she woke, she had to carry the bucket down the rear stairs, and empty the contents over the roots of the fruit trees in the garden. Every Monday, she had to wash the household's laundry by hand. It was all placed in a large tin basin under the standpipe in the yard. There, Joan would squat on a low stool with a bar of soap and washboard, scrubbing each item until her fingers were red and swollen, while her mother stood over her and screamed instructions. If she did not do something correctly, her mother would slap her shoulders and make her do it again. Joan would hang her head to conceal her tears. When she went to the clothes line to hang out the washing, her mother followed her. Joan was barely tall enough to reach the line, but her mother did not help her, just threatened to whip her if she did not hang out everything properly. Then Joan had to iron everything, under the same method of supervision.

After school, her brothers and sisters played. A ping-pong table was bought for the boys, and their friends came to play with them. Then they ate dinner, did their homework and went to bed. Joan was not allowed to play; as soon as she returned from school she had to help in the shop. On Saturdays, she swept and cleaned the bedrooms and living room and polished the floor. On Sundays, she swept and cleaned the shop. Lorna would sit and watch Joan work, never offering to help her because their mother would not permit it. For her to do anything but study and excel in mathematics was a distraction. This was how it would be for Lorna in the future as a professional middle-class person with wealth and privilege. The two boys, Andrew and Phillip, though they were not particularly bright pupils, but well-behaved and obedient, were not allowed to do any housework or run errands either. Despite the unfairness, none of her siblings came to Joan's aid – they were afraid of displeasing their mother – and expected Joan to wait on them like a servant.

Mary knew her unhappy childhood haunted her and that she needed to shake off its influence, but she did not see that it haunted her so much that she could not resist inflicting the same suffering on Joan. It did not even occur to her that this was what she was doing. She was only aware that she felt compelled to do it. From the moment that Joan was born, even though Clarice Chung was not there to pronounce judgement on whether Joan would be Chinese enough to accomplish great things, in Mary's mind this question hung over Joan's future. She returned again and again to her childhood, and thought for the first time for years about her abandonment by her father. As far as she was concerned, she was motherless, too, since her mother had been forced to give her away. The nearest thing to a mother she'd ever had was Evadne Williams, who beat and abused her.

When Joan was born, Mary knew she did not have the same maternal feelings for her as for Lorna, but Joan's aunts greeted her arrival with love and affection. They held her, cuddled and kissed her and marvelled at her in a way that Mary could not. When their mother, Susan, also came to see Joan and made a fuss of her, it made Mary angry because she could not believe that Susan was capable of loving and looking after a child. She felt revulsion seeing her mother holding Joan, felt anger, even hatred towards her. She never admitted this resentment to her mother, and could not see that she had transferred it to Joan.

If Mary did not understand herself, Joan's behaviour puzzled others. She was evidently a bright child, but seemed to have an unreasoning dislike of mathematics and her teachers could not understand why. They did not realise it was because Joan had seen the unhappiness it caused her sister, the enormous weight of expectation placed on her. From the age of five, Lorna had become a kind of celebrity, an attraction. People travelled to Canefield to see her; they would wait until Lorna returned from school, just to look at her and speculate on how she had come to possess such a remarkable brain. What did her parents feed her? Mary enjoyed these discussions and entertained the visitors with all kinds of ideas about why her eldest daughter was such a genius.

"Is her Chinese blood," Mary would say; "her father mother, Clarice Chung, was a real Chinee. She come from China with her whole family, all of them was real Chinee people; they had royal blood…" and she would remind them of the Chung's success in Georgetown, and how Lorna's Chinee grandmother say that she was going to take after them Chung.

People would ask, "What about you other pickney? They ain't take after them Chung too?"

Mary would say, "No, none of them take after them Chung, only Lorna."

This puzzled the visitors and they concluded that the difference must have been something that Mary fed Lorna. Mary didn't believe this, but she was also a shrewd shopkeeper, so she would tell them it was the cod liver oil she sold in the shop; they should purchase some too and their children might also become geniuses.

Joan accepted that Lorna was her mother's favourite, but she also knew that she always came first in spelling, vocabulary and comprehension tests. Her skills in reading made her a thoughtful and observant child with a core of confidence that nothing could shake. When Mary chastised Joan for faults she found in her housework, it was mostly like water off a duck's back.

Sometimes, though, Mary realised that she'd hurt Joan and made her weep and then she saw something of herself in her daughter; it reminded her how she had developed the strength to bear the brunt of Evadne Williams' cruelty. It reassured her that the hard work in the house was causing no real harm; Joan would grow stronger on it. However, Mary did not see the damage being done to Lorna by the enormous expectations she had placed on her.

At nights, Lorna would stay up late to do homework or mathematical exercises in preparation for the scholarship exams. When the lamplight was failing, Joan would clean the lamps and trim the wicks for her. She could see that Lorna was stressed and unhappy, sometimes weeping. Joan did not like to see this, and felt glad she was not like her sister, just pleased to have the talents she had.

When she was eleven years old, Lorna won a scholarship to St. Rose's High School, and the time came for her to leave for Georgetown. Her Uncle Harold and Auntie Lily were now settled there, with a shop of their own, and five children. Lorna would live with them, and Mary would pay them for her board and lodging.

Lorna's departure for Georgetown changed nothing for Joan; she continued to do housework, help in the shop and attend school where she continued to excel in reading and writing. But as the years passed, one teacher, Ronald Ragbir, was so impressed by Joan's abilities that he felt she should also have a secondary education, so he visited Joan's parents to tell them that Joan should sit the entrance test for secondary school, but Mary told him that she could not afford to pay the school fees for Joan, so it was out of the question.

Ronald Ragbir saw the injustice of Joan's position. He had almost lost out on furthering his own education, but he had motivated himself to go out to work at a young age, securing work as a clerk in the administrative office and at the dispensary on the estate. He had used his earnings to pay teachers at Berbice High School to prepare him privately for the scholarship examinations that would qualify him to study for a degree in English. He had realised his ambitions, gone to university in Trinidad and gained his degree; then he had returned to Canefield to teach at St. Peter's. Now he told Joan about his own struggle and how he could help her have a better future than the one her mother planned for her. She was capable of doing more than running the shop. She, too, could study for a degree, and he was prepared to help her to do this because he did not want to see her talent go to waste. She should come to his home for private lessons after school and he would prepare her to sit the GCE 'O' level examinations. He could coach her to pass the exams, since he himself had done it. It could be done in secret, without her mother's knowledge; she could tell her mother that she was going to the library to do her homework. Joan agreed to this because she liked and respected Ronald Ragbir and had enjoyed being in his class.

Ronald lived with his parents in the next village, Lucius, near the sugar estate library. She had visited his home before, to borrow books from his personal library, which he made available to the pupils who enjoyed reading. His parents lived in the upper storey of their house, and Ronald lived on the ground floor. As well as his living quarters, he had a small room where he kept his books and gave private lessons in English. Each Thursday, Joan went to his house. There, she joined a class of three boys whose parents were paying for their lessons. There was a Portuguese boy, Terry Comacho, whose father was an overseer on the estate, an Indian boy, David Doodnauth, whose father was a boilerman in the sugar factory, and a black boy, Nick Edwards, whose mother was in New York, where she worked as a nurse and sent back money to Nick's grandmother, with whom he lived. The parents of these boys could afford to buy their children all the books they needed, so they were well read, with their own libraries at home. Together, they formed a lively, enthusiastic class that Joan enjoyed very much.

There were other moves to help Joan. Her aunties, Sally and Jean, had long noticed Mary's ill-treatment of Joan and began a campaign to help her. Joan would sometimes overhear when they tried to intervene on her behalf.

Jean would say, "Oh Mary, you treating Joan too bad. The girl does work so hard for you but you never satisfied."

And Sally would add, "Joan is such a good child. She helps with the housework and in the shop, and the boys don't do any work. Mary, you are lucky to have such a helpful, hard-working daughter."

Her aunties also tried to explain to Joan why her mother was so hard on her.

They told her how when she was a child, Mary had a very difficult life, how their mother sent her away to live with a woman who treated her bad and made her work very hard, how she really suffer with this woman. Jean said, "We used to visit Mary and she used to cry and beg us to tell Mother to bring her home but Mother couldn't afford to look after all of us, so she left Mary there for four years."

At first, Joan wondered why they were telling her this. She knew it was wrong for her mother to treat her badly and felt that nothing excused it. But then what her aunts told her about Mary's childhood made her mother's behaviour interesting. She liked to read novels, particularly those where she found the characters' psychology interesting, and she liked to discuss their complexities and motivations in her classes. She almost began to treat Mary as if she was a fictional character to whom she was not related and whose behaviour did not affect her. But Mary was not a fictional character; she was very real and Joan could not cut herself off from her entirely, however much she tried to stay detached. She pitied the child Mary had been, moreso when her aunties talked about their absent father, James Abdul. They told her that of all Susan's children, Mary looked most like the father who had abandoned them. It was his fault their mother had given Mary to Evadne

Williams. Perhaps it was because Mary looked so much like him that their mother chose her to send away, because she did not want to be reminded of him. Joan knew her aunts were asking her not to judge her mother, but to forgive and love her, but felt no one had to teach her to do this.

Joan's aunties also felt that something practical must be done to help Mary and Joan, so they suggested that their mother, Susan, should come and live at Canefield. With an extra pair of hands to help with the housework and in the shop, the stress would be taken off both of them. This seemed a simple and straightforward solution, but it exposed another layer of complication in Joan's and Mary's lives – adding to Joan's perplexity about how she should respond to the letters she began to receive from Lorna. The letters confirmed what Joan already suspected, that Lorna hated the burden of expectations placed on her, and wished to reject it, that she got no pleasure or satisfaction from their mother's favour. She was very unhappy at St. Rose's school; she hated living with Uncle Harold and Auntie Lily; her life in Georgetown was so stressful it was making her ill; she was suffering from bronchitis and asthma; she wanted to return home and stop studying.

SUSAN LEO

When Susan arrived to live with them, she set about making herself useful at once. At nights and on weekends, she made brown paper bags and sweets for the shop. She began to create a vegetable garden. She bought chickens and ducks that she looked after lovingly. She gave them names, talked to them and nursed them when they were ill. Susan helped Joan with all her chores, and they quickly formed a close bond. As her aunts had intended, it did help Joan to have Susan around, because Susan became a shield against Mary's bullying. But when Susan displayed her affection for Joan openly and cooked special treats for her like stuffed karila, Mary could not help thinking that when she was a child she had never received such loving kindness.

Susan told Joan that her grandfather, James Abdul, was still alive and living in Georgetown, but he was very ill in hospital where he was having a leg amputated because he had diabetes. Susan wanted to take Joan to meet him before he died, and a day was set aside for them to make the visit, Joan's first trip to the capital.

On the day of their journey, Joan and Susan rose before dawn. They bathed in lamplight, had a small breakfast, then stood in the darkness at the roadside to wait for the first bus to arrive, observing the eerie shapes of sugar workers emerging out of the mist to set off for the fields.

Joan felt adventurous and very close to Susan. Every step of the journey to Georgetown to meet her mysterious grandfather was exciting, sometimes alarming, as on the ferry crossing of the Berbice River. The currents were strong and the boat rocked; they had to stand on the crowded lower level of the boat, in the middle of a crowd of farmers and hucksters with their bags and baskets of produce. It was cold and windy and Joan stood tightly by Susan. It was even more exciting to board the train, feel its engine shudder into life, then hear the shrill whistle that sent it on its way. As it gathered speed and hurtled forward, Joan was so excited she could not keep still; she swung her feet, wriggled and fidgeted, and leaned out the window to look at the passing scenery.

In Georgetown, it was obvious that Susan knew the place well, but Joan feared that if she did not keep close to her grandmother she would be lost. They took a bus to George-town Hospital, and there Joan got the feeling that it was not Susan's first visit to see James Abdul. She did not ask anyone the way, but walked straight to his bedside. What first struck Joan was how handsome he was. He looked like an aging Indian film star, like a grey-haired Dilip Kumar, whose face she knew from the giant posters that advertised his films at the *Tajmahal* cinema. He smiled at Joan, opened his arms, and hugged and kissed her. She then sat on the chair beside his bed, next to Susan. Susan leaned forward to be close to him, and they talked to each other for about ten minutes. Joan noticed that while they talked, they held hands under his pillow, and there were tears in their eyes. Joan could see that under the sheets his right leg was missing. When they finally left him, Joan saw that Susan was very sad, wiping the tears from her cheeks. In spite of their unhappy history, she knew they still loved each other.

James Abdul signalled Joan to come closer, and he said, "*I* am your grandfather; my name is James Abdul; I came from Kashmir." He emphasised *I*, and tapped his hairy chest, as if to say he was the only man who could possibly be her grandfather.

This puzzled Joan, but later that day, she understood why her grandfather had spoken this way. Susan had taken her to the room in Albuoystown where she had once lived with James Abdul, and where, after he abandoned her, she had continued to live with their six children. It was with a sense of wonder that Joan stepped into the room where her mother and her aunts had lived. It felt like being in the past, but the man who was living there now was not from the past. Susan told Joan that his name was Motilall; he had come from India only two years ago and did not speak English well; he worked at Stabroek market as a porter, which was where they met when he started to help her at her stall. They had become friends and he had moved in with her. Jean and Sally had met him, her mother knew about him but had not met him; he would be returning to Canefield with them to meet Mary, and he would be staying for a week. Then he would visit her for a week every month; it had been arranged with her mother.

.   Susan and Motilall took Joan to Stabroek market so she could see the stall where Susan had earned her living for many years. Motilall filled a jute sack with the best fruits he could find – his present for Mary – then they caught a bus to the train station.

On the way home, Joan thought how it was like the plots of the Indian movies at the *Tajmahal*. She discovered that Susan had chosen the romance of an Indian identity and loved Indian culture and two Indian men. Joan had heard rumours about this aspect of Susan's life from her aunties and mother – that at the market Susan had become part of the community of Indian peasant farmers who brought their produce from the Essequibo islands, the East Coast and the

East Bank to Georgetown. She spoke Hindi and dressed in saris to go to the cinema with them. She had learned to cook Indian food. Susan only looked Chinese; she behaved like an Indian. Her daughters spoke disparagingly about this.

When they arrived at Canefield, it was obvious that Mary did not welcome Motilall's presence. He eagerly presented her with his gift of fruits, but she pretended not to care. He peeled and served her a fruit salad, but she did not eat any of it. All week she treated him coldly.

Motilall shared Susan's bedroom. They left the door open so it was easy to see them sleeping in bed together, with their arms around each other. They bathed together, sat in the garden drying and combing each other's hair, and massaging each other's hands and feet with coconut oil. It irritated Mary that they sat in a part of the garden where they could be seen by passers-by. She told them they were making a spectacle of themselves, and asked them not to massage each other in the garden where everyone could see them. But there was no hiding their relationship; they liked to go to the cinema together and walked there holding hands; in the cinema Motilall even put his arm around Susan while they watched the film. She would wear a sari, all her jewellery, and place a red bindi dot on her forehead, the symbol of a married Hindu woman. People who saw them came to the shop to tease Mary; they called Motilall and Susan "dulahin" and "dulaha", bride and bridegroom.

Another irritation was that Motilall did not like to use toilet paper; instead he kept soap and water in the latrine for his own use; Mary disapproved of this and threw the soap and bottle away. She insisted he must use toilet paper. She did not like it either when he appeared in the shop with Susan and tried to help her there. He must keep out of the shop; he could not speak English, so no one understood him.

Jean and Sally visited Mary to see how she was getting

on with Motilall. They told Joan that they were not surprised that Mary detested him, since he encouraged their mother in her Indian ways.

Joan did not dislike Motilall; she thought he was kind and loving and brought a rare happiness into their home. She liked it that he and Susan did everything together; they looked after the garden, tended the chickens and ducks, and cooked – all together. Joan had never seen such a loving relationship between a couple, and it shocked her that Susan's daughters were not happy to see them together.

Jean told Joan that they resented Susan's love of Indian men and culture because it had blighted their lives; she had made a bad choice when she chose James Abdul; he was a curse on them, he had caused their deprivation and suffering; they could never forgive their mother for this. Mary felt this most strongly; it was an insult that her mother could bring Motilall to her home and flaunt their relationship in her face. She told her sisters that she would tell Motilall he must not come to her home again.

When she told Motilall this, he and Susan did not try to change her mind, and he left quietly, with the empty jute sack slung across his shoulders.

It was after Motilall left that Joan was able to observe that Susan and Mary always tried to avoid each other. When Susan was in one part of the shop making paper bags, Mary would stay in a different part; they would glance at each other, then quickly look away. Susan liked to cook, but whatever she cooked Mary never ate, eating only what their servant prepared. Mary did not try to hide her dislike of her mother. If any of the customers tried to strike up a conversation with Susan, Mary would discourage it.

Susan sought solace with Joan. She treated Joan like a small child, would sit her in the garden to brush her hair and give her manicures and pedicures and do her chores for her.

"You making she lazy!" Mary would snap, and it made her very angry when Susan took Joan to the cinema to see Indian movies. "You want she turn into a coolie like you!"

The stress of living with Mary's hostility began to take its toll on Susan and she became ill. She lost her appetite, and took to her bed where she would cry out in pain. Frederick called for the doctor who sent Susan to the hospital for tests that revealed that she was suffering from bowel cancer that was too advanced for treatment. The doctor told them that it was inevitable that Susan would die in a few months; all he could suggest was that she be given aspirin for the pain; there was nothing he could do for her.

Even this crisis did not make Mary show any compassion for her mother; it made her even more distant and detached. When Susan cried out in pain, Mary refused to go to her and sent Joan or her sons instead, to give her aspirins and water.

Jean and Sally came to visit Susan. They brought her soups that they made especially for her, and new nightgowns to make her more comfortable. They wept over her and spoke affectionately to her. Mary would find an excuse to absent herself when they were there.

On the day that Susan died, Joan was sitting with her and she sensed that she was fading away. She asked Susan if she wanted Mary, but she shook her head, turned away and gazed outside at the blue skies overhead. The window was wide open; the breeze that rustled the leaves of the mango tree that grew near the room blew on Susan and ruffled the wisps of hair on her forehead. She blinked away her tears and squeezed Joan's hand. Then her head fell to one side as she breathed her last breath. Joan called Mary and she came upstairs slowly, stood by her mother's bed and looked at her, but said nothing. Joan felt caught between them: Susan who lay dead on the bed, her life silenced, and her mother who stood above them, looking down at them both with a look of abandonment and desperation on her face. Mary went downstairs to tell Frederick that Susan was dead, then sent a message to her sisters to let them know.

That night, her daughters sat around the corpse and talked in whispers about their mother. Joan sat with them and listened to them repeat the familiar stories – what a terrible life Susan had lived, poor parents, orphaned at four – no one knew when she was born, or the names of her parents – how she'd been taken in by Chinese people but forced to work for her keep; how she met James Abdul and had children for him but he left her and went to live with another woman; how she struggled hard to raise her children alone and took up with the Indian farmers at Stabroek market who taught her to be Indian – how she liked being an Indian and did not want to be Chinese like Clarice Chung

The mention of Clarice Chung always made Joan tense. They brought her up only when they wanted to compare their mother negatively with her. They said that Clarice Chung was a better woman than their mother; she came from a wealthy, successful family who looked after their children; she had the ambition their mother lacked.

It made Joan sad to see Susan's cheap coffin while her daughters sat around it, unable to say anything good or loving about her. She felt the injustice and unfairness of it. She wanted to defend Susan's memory because she loved her. Susan had treated her kindly and lovingly. She had gone to Indian movies with her and saw how they made Susan's eyes light up and shine in the dark, because of the tears she wept. If she had dared to speak, Joan would have told them that Susan was not just a poor woman with a history of deprivation and abandonment, but a woman of deep feelings, who loved deeply and genuinely, who though she never had money or material things to give, had plenty of love. Joan wanted to tell them she was certain that their mother loved them all, especially Mary, the one she felt she had failed, who herself believed that her mother had given her nothing, who believed that Clarice Chung was a better woman because she gave her a shop, and made her a successful shopkeeper. That was the best thing anyone had given her – the shop that gave her a home and money of her own; the shop that she wished to pass on to Joan; the shop that Clarice Chung had given her while her own mother, Susan Leo, had given her nothing.

The sisters decided that they would not let Motilall know that Susan had died; they did not want him to come to her funeral; they did not want him in their lives. It was wrong for Susan to have a relationship with him; he was just an illiterate labourer from India; it was a disgrace how they were so old and behaved like young lovers. They said that perhaps it was he who caused her death, by carrying on with her as if they were young lovers; he was to blame for her cancer.

They agreed that they would give their mother a Christian burial in St. Peter's graveyard, in a corner reserved for their family, where Clarice Chung was buried; they would bury her next to Clarice. They told Joan that her two Chinese grandmothers would lie there in the graveyard together, and when she went there, she could pay her respects to both of them. Joan did not like them burying Susan next to Clarice Chung. She deduced from what her aunts had told her that Clarice Chung was not a nice person, she was a terrible snob who had too high an opinion of herself and her clan; she had treated them badly. They had told Joan that when Mary and Lily became her daughters-in-law, she had ill-treated them; she had thrown hot food at Lily and threatened to kill her; she was a cruel and

103

vicious woman who rejected them for not being fully Chinese. Why, then, Joan wondered, did they profess to respect Clarice Chung and not their own mother? Joan felt the terrible injustice of it, and when they went to the funeral to bury Susan Leo next to Clarice Chung, she refused to go and witness it; she preferred to sit in the garden that Susan had created while she lived with them.

The mango tree was full of ripe fruit. There were bunches of bananas to be picked, and guava, corn, pepper and squash on the vines. Joan sat and looked at the fruits of Susan's labour and felt her presence there in her garden. The chickens she loved and gave names to pecked around her feet. On the ground there were still the grains of rice and corn that Susan had scattered when she last fed them; the fowls were missing her, and so was she. Her mother and aunts had told her that she had two Chinese grandmothers but she felt strongly that she only had one, the one she would always remember with love and affection, Susan Leo.

There was only one possession that Susan prized – a small, blue-glass lamp that Joan used to help her clean and light when darkness fell, and she decided that she would claim ownership of this lamp and keep it until she too died.

Joan also claimed the room that Susan had lived in for her own, and there she kept the books and papers she was studying for the G.C.E. examinations; she kept the door locked so that Mary would not find out. She missed Susan badly but did not dwell on her grief because there was no time. She continued to work hard at the housework and in the shop, and she did not let Mary's difficult behaviour trouble her. Her secret life at Ronald Ragbir's private school was too interesting and this kept her busy and preoccupied.

In the school vacations, Lorna returned home and repeated to Joan how unhappy she was in Georgetown. She felt isolated at school because all the Chinese girls there came from wealthy families; only she came from a rural shop. The teenage culture of England and America dominated Georgetown; all the girls wore the latest overseas fashions; their parents owned Cadillac and De Soto cars and drove their daughters to school and collected them. She said that when she visited the homes of these wealthy girls, she saw how much better they lived; she did not eat well at Uncle Harold's and Auntie Lily's home.

Joan tried to reassure Lorna, telling her that she had nothing to be ashamed of since she was the brightest girl in the school, but this did not console Lorna; she felt her intelligence was just a burden. When it was time for her to return to school, Lorna wept and told her parents that she did not want to return to Georgetown, but stay at home like Joan. Mary told Lorna how lucky she was, she could not understand her unhappiness, but she would send Joan to see her off; Joan would cross the river with her and wait on the train with her until it was time for it to depart. Joan left Lorna weeping with sorrow on the train. She did not tell Lorna that she was secretly studying for G.C.E 'O' level exams, and she returned home sensing the irony of their difference.

NEW DAYS AND DEPARTURES

Times were changing rapidly in the country. The first big political party, the People's Progressive Party, led by Cheddi Jagan, had split in two, and the conflict between the two sides, Indians and Africans, was tearing the country apart. People said Cheddi Jagan was causing uproar with his communist politics. He wanted to rid the country of Bookers, the British company that ran the sugar estates; he wanted an end to British rule and the British to leave the country; his opponents said that he wanted British Guiana to become a communist country, with him as prime minister, that his wife was a communist, too. Together, they campaigned for independence and made fiery speeches that alarmed the British and American governments. When he had first come to power, when Joan was only a small girl, the British had been so alarmed, they had sent in their army and warships, and locked up Jagan and his supporters.

Now politics was dividing people in the rural areas from people in the towns, and dividing the races. Africans saw Jagan as coming from the rural sugar estates, and caring only about the Indians. He spoke the language of communism, and this turned the business communities of Georgetown and New Amsterdam against him. Politics split between Jagan, the Indian, and Forbes Burnham, the African. When the Portuguese businessman, Peter D'Aguiar, entered politics and formed a new party, the United Force, he attracted the support of the other races, especially the

Portuguese, and this further split the country along racial lines. It was all the customers spoke about when Joan was serving in the shop.

Even in Ronald Ragbir's class, the pupils became politically divided by race. Nick Edwards's mother sent him books about the Black struggle in the United States and he became obsessed with it. He identified himself as a supporter of Forbes Burnham and his People's National Congress. He and David Doodnauth fell out, because David's father was a member of Jagan's People's Progressive Party. David was hoping that in a few years he would receive a scholarship from the party to study medicine in Russia. Jagan's opponents claimed that under his leadership, the country would be taken over by Russia. In the middle of all this, Lorna won a scholarship to study Economics in England.

The preparation for Lorna's departure to England was feverish. Mary took the whole family to New Amsterdam to buy a suitcase for her. She asked the St. Rose's teachers to arrange for Lorna to get a British passport, and help her to buy a few items of warm clothing. When Lorna came home with these things, Mary spread them out on the shop counter like trophies for everyone to see. Women in the shop joked that Mary was behaving as if Lorna was going to England for her coronation.

Little by little, Lorna's suitcase was packed, and on the day of her flight, the whole family set off for the ferry in a hired car. Auntie Jean and Sally went too, in their best clothes. It took five hours for them to arrive at Atkinson airport by ferry, train and taxis. When they reached the airport, they saw that many other students from the rural areas were also leaving to study overseas. Whole families and neighbours had come in country buses, some of them wailing with grief as if they were never going to see the departing students again. Mary, though, was certain that Lorna was going to return home to look after her, so she did not shed a tear.

When the time came for the departees to walk to their planes, some of their relatives screamed and fainted, but Lorna walked across the tarmac in a calm and dignified manner. She did not look back, not until she was at the top of the aircraft stairs, when she turned around, waved, then ducked into the plane. Mary jumped up and down and waved while the BOAC Boeing jet turned on the runway, then sped along and soared into the sky with a mighty roar that made them cover their ears. Then there was silence and the airport emptied as people returned to their cars and buses and drove away.

On the drive back to Canefield, they all wept a little. Though planned for many years, it still came as a shock to Joan that Lorna could be swept away from them so suddenly, taken to a place they knew about only from photographs in the newspapers and magazines, and from the movies. Although Lorna had not lived at home for many years, Georgetown was only a few hours travel, but now her sister had gone thousands of miles away, many hours' plane journey, a journey that required passports and clothing she did not have. Lorna had gone to a place that might turn her into a stranger. Perhaps she would return speaking like an English person and looking like one. They said the winter cold turned your skin white; Lorna's skin was already pale; the winter would make it whiter; she would return like a white ghost – and maybe different, no longer her big sister. It felt as if Lorna had died and she would never see her again, and even if she did, she would not be the same.

But Joan had set herself the goal of passing her 'O' level

exams, so she put aside her sadness and returned to her studies, though she had begun to wonder what she was studying for. Lorna had gone to England while she was left to live in British Guiana with all the political confusion and uncertainty about its future. Could she believe what Ronald Ragbir said? He read magazines, newspapers and books from America and England and it made him excited about the future. He said the world was changing and he told Joan that she was living in exciting times when nations were ending colonialism and becoming independent; women and black people would be free; there were going to be revolutionary technological and scientific changes; computers and science would change the world for the better; people would travel to the moon. She was going to live in a world her ancestors could not dream of, she was lucky to be born when she was. Listen to the music coming out of America and England, he told her, and she would hear how free the world was becoming. He bought these records and played them for her, the songs of Bob Dylan, and Joan Baez especially. He played Bob Dylan singing "The Times They are a Changing" and she memorised the words and sang them to herself.

But Ronald Ragbir's conviction that they must prepare to live in a new and better world bemused Joan since she could not see any future for herself, apart from working in the shop on the sugar estate. At home, her parents worried about the politics of the country, especially how Cheddi Jagan, with his Communist ideas, was still engaging in conflict with the British and American governments. They had imprisoned him before and sent in their armies to overthrow him. Now they were trying to remove him from power again. This was causing difficulties on the sugar estates. There were strikes and shutdowns and in Georgetown rioters had set fire to Water Street, the business centre. Later, there were race riots in Georgetown between Africans and Indians and this conflict spread across the country, so that the two groups began to separate and live in divided areas, even in Canefield where the Black people moved to Dorset while the Indian people stayed in Canefield. Because of the chaos and confusion, people began to leave the country, planning never to return. It seemed that the country was doomed. Lorna's departure looked increasingly like a good thing; she was safe, far away in England. Mary now hoped that one day, when she finished her degree, Lorna would help the entire family to leave the country and live in England, but in the meantime, she would have to rely on Joan to help them.

Joan passed her G.C.E 'O' level exams in English Language, English Literature, History, Religious Education, Latin and French. When she told her parents about it, to her surprise her mother was delighted and at once asked Ronald Ragbir to help her write an application for a job at the bank in New Amsterdam she'd seen advertised in the newspaper, and offered him payment to write the letter. With all the political troubles, Mary felt there was no future for them in keeping the shop, and since Joan had shown she could do better, a job as a bank clerk would earn a good salary and Joan would be able to look after them. Ronald Ragbir helped Joan write the letter of application, and he, Mary and Joan, took the letter to the bank in New Amsterdam and delivered it straight to the manager and waited for him to read it. To their delight, the manager invited Joan into his office and interviewed her. It was a brief and friendly interview and he offered her a job, starting the next month. Although it had never been Joan's idea to work in a bank, she felt a sense of pride and accomplishment because such jobs were difficult to obtain, and it seemed to be on wings that she travelled back to Canefield on the bus. Mary had often talked about how, when she was a child in Georgetown, she would go to look at the Chinese girls in the nearby bank, impressed by how pretty and clever they seemed. Joan was not used to being seen as a clever Chinese girl, but she was relieved to be free of her destiny to inherit the shop, like her mother, and Clarice Chung.

In the weeks before starting her new job, Joan gave up going to her lessons with Ronald Ragbir, and to borrow his books and magazines. She visited the bank to collect her uniform, stopping to look at the people she would be working with. The Portuguese, Chinese and Indian girls looked so very modern, glamorous and sophisticated; they wore hairstyles in the latest British and American fashions. It made her anxious to look like them, and on her way to get the bus back to Canefield, she stopped at the hairdresser in Main Street to ask how much it would cost to get such a sixties hairstyle. It was so expensive she told the hairdresser it would have to wait until she received her first salary.

When she walked into the bank on her first day, Joan felt so numb with fear it was difficult to place one foot in front of the other. She was afraid to open her mouth to speak, so she said nothing if she could help it.

The manager, Mr. Evans, a kindly Welshman with a twinkle in his eye, seemed sympathetic, as if he could see how nervous she was. He smiled when he spoke to welcome her, then introduced her to the staff, telling them to look after her and teach her the ropes. Playfully, he threatened that if anyone mistreated her, he would sack them. He called her "the new girl" and told her that if she needed help, "Yell , and I'll come!" Then he disappeared into his office. The Chief Accountant told her she was on counter

111

duty. As customers came in, he showed her how to open a new savings account and how to fill in various forms, then he left her to stand at the counter, where her anxiety multiplied by the second. She was certain that everyone could see that she knew nothing, so she tried to mimic the other girls by attempting to sound like them when they spoke in their perfect English, and tried to stride around as confidently as they did. Whenever she had to ask for help she burned with shame because she could see how they regarded her with pity. The next day was the same, but little by little she learned to accomplish each task and her confidence built, so by the end of the month she felt it was natural for her to work there.

When a bank account was opened for her in her own name and her first month's salary was paid in there, she felt extremely wealthy. She went home and told Mary what she had been paid and her mother told her she must give her fifty dollars each month for her board and lodging. Mary said nothing else but Joan knew it meant a great deal to her mother to receive this support. The shop brought in very little profit, and what it made had to be reinvested in new stock. How they managed to pay the high school fees for her two brothers Joan couldn't imagine; she knew her parents struggled to buy meat, fish and vegetables for their meals and keep their family decently clothed. Mary sewed all the family's clothes with Clarice's old sewing machine, buying the cheapest fabrics, though she got the latest British and American patterns and was a skilful seamstress. There were smart dresses to be bought off-the-peg at the Bookers store in town, dresses shipped in from England, and Mary would try to match them with dresses she made at home. Joan's contribution to their finances was the biggest boost they had ever received. Mary began to show Joan a respect she had never shown her before. No more urine bucket to empty in the morning. Now, Mary employed a young Indian girl to do the housework, and each morning she provided Joan with a breakfast of bacon, eggs, and toast before she departed for the bank.

After a few months Joan gained enough skill and confidence to be promoted to the job of cashier, and found herself in control of a till of thousands of dollars daily, more money than her parents had ever seen in their lives. Lorna was studying economics at university in England, but Joan was learning it hands-on in the bank.

Lorna continued to write to Joan, confiding her secrets, just as when she was at school in Georgetown. She was not happy in London. She missed home, especially the food; it was too cold and damp; the scholarship money was not enough to live on; she could not afford to buy warm clothing; the hall where she lived was chilly and over-crowded; she was always ill with colds, flu and asthma, and England had given her bronchitis, too. In short, she was miserable and hated England.

There were no complaints in the letters Joan wrote to Lorna. She enjoyed her job and it satisfied her to help her parents. She went to work each morning with her head held high. Now, she too strode around the bank with confidence. Yet there was something missing in her life – the reading she used to do and even the writing of essays – and it was this feeling of emptiness that made her visit Ronald Ragbir one Saturday morning, a year after she joined the bank. She found him there with his old students, Nick Edwards, Terry Comacho, and David Doodnauth. They had passed their 'O' level exams and were now studying for 'A' levels so they could go to university in Jamaica and Russia. There was, too, the new University of Guyana where it was possible to attend evening courses while you worked in the day; now it was not necessary to get a scholarship to go to England like Lorna. Ronald was right, the world had changed for the better, in spite of the political turmoil. The country was now independent; Cheddi Jagan had been deposed and Forbes Burnham was the new Prime Minister. As Ronald Ragbir had predicted, the black people in the country felt free. Joan could see the change in Nick Edwards. He now wore his hair in the radical Afro style, used Black Power slang and was always raising his fist in a salute to emphasise a point. Joan thought he had become arrogant with his new ideology and she hated the way he looked her up and down as if undressing her with his eyes and spoke sarcastically to her, calling her "chick". He told her that she had sold out by working at a foreign capitalist bank. She told him she had done nothing of the sort; working at the bank enabled her to look after her family, and this was a necessity. She was not a capitalist, she was a socialist like her parents and had supported Cheddi Jagan because he was for the liberation of the sugar estate workers. Nick shook his head and said that Jagan was a racist; he did not look after black people, only the Indians; he supported Forbes Burnham because he was black. David Doodnauth disagreed with him and the two of them argued ferociously, even with hatred. For Joan it was proof of how race had divided the country and because of this she hoped she could find a way of leaving and never returning.

She looked at the new books on Ronald's shelves. They were full of the Utopian ideas of the sixties – the Beat writers, and the works of Marshall McLuhan. He was now full of the youth counter-culture of England and the United States. He told Joan that Lorna was living at an exciting time there in London and she should visit her to experience this for herself; on her return, she should rejoin him for 'A' level lessons and then join Lorna at university in London because it was such a great time to be young and alive. There in swinging London women were being liberated by the birth-control pill and the rise of feminism.

Joan noted that whilst Ronald was celebrating the end of colonialism and the birth of national independence in Guyana, he was still pointing to London as the centre of new ideas, but she said nothing. Still, some of his new books interested her and she borrowed books by Jean-Paul Sartre and Albert Camus and experienced again the excited anticipation she used to feel when she took home new authors from the library in New Amsterdam. Her love of reading had given her the escape route out of working in the shop, could it also bring her a more personal freedom?

When Mary saw her arrive with the pile of books in her arms, she asked her why she was still wasting her time reading. But not only did Joan begin to read again, she also bought a record player to listen to the records Lorna sent from London – the music of the Beatles, and other groups from America. Their lyrics were so exuberant and full of ideas, dreams and hopes. Lorna's letters began to sound more hopeful too, and this made Joan think that perhaps she should visit her. She started to look into the costs of travel to London, but meantime other possibilities were coming in her direction.

Out of the blue, a woman called Annie Chung presented herself to them one day, saying she was a distant cousin, one of the Chungs from Georgetown and she had come to reclaim Frederick, since, with deaths and departures abroad, they were the last of the Chungs. She claimed to be a cousin of Dr. Elizabeth Chung who had died and left her a large house in Camp Street, Georgetown, where she now lived alone. By coincidence, the bank manager had offered Joan a transfer to the bank's head office in Georgetown. He told her she was stuck in a rut there in Berbice and it was time for her to move on and develop her career. She should do the banking exams and set her sights on becoming a manager. Her father suggested that she should stay with Annie Chung in Georgetown, to give her company, so Joan left her home in Canefield in 1966 to live in Georgetown.

GEORGETOWN

As the bus drew away, Joan watched her mother waving from the shop. It was a relief to be leaving her behind. Memories of their relationship passed like a reel of film through her mind and she recalled the pain and sadness Mary had given her during her childhood. Now she was free from her, putting distance between them rapidly. She remembered herself as the eight-year-old whom Mary had burdened with work, as the child to whom her mother had shown no love or compassion. As the bus sped towards the ferry, that burden fell away, as if the weight of the huge tub of laundry she used to wash on Mondays had lifted from her shoulders. She had left behind her actual sufferings, but would she ever be able to erase the painful memories that just being with her mother often aroused? Had Mary ever erased from her memory those who had destroyed her childhood? Where did it end?

As she headed to the city on the ferry boat and the speeding train, Joan knew that her journey must continue further, to London in time, but first there was Georgetown to discover. Annie Chung had told Frederick that she wanted to go to China to find where their family began, but as Joan neared Georgetown, China could not have been further from her mind. She had grown up hearing only terrible things about her grandmother from China, Clarice Chung, about what a cold and racial person she was. Clarice had died before she was born, but she could not believe Annie Chung when she tried to tell her what a great thing her Chinese heritage was.

But why did she recognise Annie Chung's house as soon as she set eyes on it? It chimed with something inside her, as if she had been there before. Much later, when she thought about it, she realised it was because she had heard about this house from her aunties Jean and Sally, who had lived there when they were children. They had brought Mary to this house to show her the luxury in which wealthy Chinese women lived and from which had come Mary's dreams of the life she hoped Lorna would achieve. There was something fantastic about going to live in Elizabeth Chung's house and work in the bank where her mother and sisters had gone to gawp at the smart and clever Chinese girls they would never become.

She would miss her literary studies with Ronald Ragbir, but now, with the University of Guyana offering part-time degrees in the evening, she could fulfil her dream of studying for a degree and paying for it with the salary she would be earning. Perhaps she could get a degree here in Guyana, then go to England to live with Lorna.

Annie Chung's elegant wooden house in Camp Street was built in the grand, early nineteenth century, colonial style, with ornate Demerara shutters all around and a split-level, gabled green roof. When Annie let her in through the wide front door, Joan found herself in an expansive living-room full of large, colonial-style furniture. Its elegance was dated and faded like Annie Chung, who looked ancient and lost in it. Annie greeted her and took her to her room at the rear of the house. The house was far too large for just two of them; it felt cavernous and lonely. Joan had her own large, tiled bathroom and her room was so luxurious it made her uncomfortable. She did not belong there, felt lost in the massive space, like a floating leaf brought in on the wind of time. She had not moved into the future but into the past, from which she thought she was free when she left home.

Later, Annie came to her room to speak to her, trying to be friendly. She stood in the doorway, puffed on a cigarette and peered at Joan as if to try to focus on her, her eyesight evidently poor. She told Joan that her husband had died many years ago; he was a wealthy Chinese doctor; they had travelled all over the world, to Japan, Singapore, Hong Kong, New York, Paris, London; the house was full of souvenirs they brought back from those places; it was such a good life they used to have; here in Georgetown they used to belong to the Georgetown Club which was very exclusive; they used to play tennis with the British governor and his wife, but those days were gone; they had chased the British people out of the country; Burnham did not want people like them any more; all the middle-class people were leaving – all the Chinese and Portuguese businessmen and professionals; Burnham was taxing them too hard and showing them disrespect, so they were all selling up and leaving; maybe she should sell up and leave too; her sister lived in Canada, maybe she would go to live with her; it was the end for the country; Burnham was destroying everything; everyone was leaving; it was time to leave.

Annie was so filling her room with cigarette smoke and gloom that Joan told her she needed to go to bed and get some sleep. At last, Annie left her alone, with a reminder that she would expect her to pay seventy-five dollars a month rental for the room promptly on the last day of each month and there was a maid who came once a fortnight who would clean her room and do her laundry if she paid her.

In the morning, Joan walked to work, still thinking how remarkable it was to find herself here, with a job in the bank, and living with a descendant of the Chung family in a beautiful house in Camp Street. It was as if she immediately belonged to Georgetown; it was where the Chung family made their name, where they rose from obscurity as indentured people on Soesdyke estate to middle-class prominence. These were the people Clarice Chung had told her mother about, who had inspired Mary to dream of a better life. This was why Lorna was studying in England, so she could, as Mary had once desired, return and lift them from poverty in Canefield, and bring them to Georgetown. Instead it was she, Joan, who was there. But whose dream was it that had brought her here, she asked herself as she walked along the shady avenues of Camp and Main Street. Her mother's, not her own. Here, her other grandmother, Susan Leo, had been orphaned and suffered as a servant in the homes of Chinese people in the old Chinatown; here she had met James Abdul before he abandoned her and she'd raised their six children alone. Here, her mother and aunts had lived and dreamed and suffered. Had they belonged to Georgetown? For a moment she felt as if she was walking in their shadows and the legacy of their oppression felt heavy. But when she entered the bank and saw its beautiful interior, the heaviness lifted. It was an open, spacious two-storey colonial building. Two Doric columns framed the entrance. Inside, there was a large dome with glass panels in the roof that let in the sunlight. Around the upper storey was a circular balcony with an ornate balustrade. On the ground floor, there was a circular counter which went almost around the building, interrupted only by the cashiers' tills; within this circle the clerks sat at their desks. The two floors were connected by a wide, ornate staircase. The bank was open and busy with queues of customers. It looked very modern, comfortable and welcoming. It was not like arriving for her first day at the small bank in New Amsterdam. Then she had been over-

120

awed. Now, she had no reason to feel anxious about starting this new post. The transfer had brought an increase in salary; she would be able to save up enough money to visit London to see Lorna, as well as increase what she gave her parents. She had promised Mary she would return to visit them at the end of every month with her contribution.

In spite of her mixed feelings about the very different experiences of the two sides of her family, she found herself enjoying Georgetown. She and Annie Chung developed a polite relationship in which they lived separate and different lives. Annie spent her days running errands and shopping around the city, then at nights she stayed in her room where she listened to the radio, read and talked to herself. She had a small circle of women friends, all Chinese, who met occasionally to play mahjong in her living room; most were widows like Annie, who had also been married to wealthy professional Chinese men and left with a comfortable home and an income they had once thought they could live on for the rest of their lives.

Annie introduced Joan to them as "a Chung", and when the women nodded and smiled at her approvingly, she realised that the connection automatically conferred prestige. It was the same in the bank. It was assumed that if you were Chinese, you must be descended from family with high status. This was the class snobbery that Lorna had referred in her letters when she was at St. Rose's High School, where she had felt out of place as the daughter of poor Chinese shopkeepers from a sugar estate.

In the bank, when Joan was introduced to anyone, the inevitable question would be: "Who are your family?" and they would try to think of a Wong family who were middle-class. When Joan told them she was not related to any living Wongs in Georgetown, this was evidently difficult to believe. When she told people that she had grown up on a sugar estate in Berbice, where her family were shopkeepers, they quickly lost interest in her. She knew that if she wanted to impress anyone, she could do it by citing her Chung ancestry, but she chose not to do this and found herself not being invited to parties or being drawn into any of their social circles. The new politics was complicating it, but enough of the old hierarchies of race, wealth and culture survived in the codes of snobbery that controlled relationships in Georgetown.

The people who worked in the bank understood these codes and negotiated the new complications expertly. Joan learned to recognise this code but she did not wish to live by it. Perhaps you had to have grown up in Georgetown to feel comfortable with these rules, though her mother and aunties had evidently been oppressed by them. She did not make friends at the bank or enter into the social life of her colleagues, feeling she did not belong among them. She felt she belonged only when she returned at the end of the month to Canefield to visit her family and bring them her financial contribution.

She also visited Ronald Ragbir because she missed him and his good influence, especially his love of books, the culture of discussion and debate and his knowledge of the latest developments in modern literature in the U.S. and England. Ronald told her that his former pupils had passed their 'A' level exams. David Doodnauth had left for Russia to study medicine, Terry Comacho was planning to study in Toronto, and Nick Edwards hoped to go to university in Trinidad. She, too, should study for a degree, enrol at the University of Guyana to study English; she could do it part-time, in the evenings. He himself was planning to move to Georgetown to study for a Master's in Politics and Government because he wanted to have a career in politics, which excited him more than teaching.

When Ronald did move to Georgetown, his rented room in Albertown was not very far from where Joan was living. He worked part-time as a teacher at Central High School, and he took in students for private lessons. She visited to borrow and discuss books with him and enjoyed renewing their friendship, though she was worried about his consuming interest in politics. She also enrolled at the university to study for a degree in English, and found herself enjoying her studies far more than working in the bank.

Forbes Burnham, the prime minister, despite having come to power with American support, was now practising his own form of cooperative socialism that included plans to nationalise the banks and other sectors of the economy. In the fifties and sixties, people had begun to flee the country to escape from Cheddi Jagan's communism and the racial conflicts that followed. Now, they were fleeing from Forbes Burnham's brand of socialism. Many people from the bank emigrated. Some of Annie Chung's mah-jong friends went to Canada because of the difficulties their businesses were facing, as the government inflicted crippling taxes on them.

Without her friends, Annie became crotchety and irritable. She would pace up and down her empty house at night and complain about conditions in the country. She would grumble to Joan that all the best business people had gone, all the Chinese and Portuguese people who ran the businesses in this country, all going away because Burnham was persecuting them. He was making rules that made it impossible for them to run their businesses; he was destroying this country; everybody running away. She was going to go to Canada, too. The country was good for nothing; everybody going away.

LONDON

In 1968, Joan decided to visit Lorna in London. She would go for one month. She took paid leave, set up a bank account for Mary, and arranged for the monthly sum to be paid to her while she was away. Unlike so many others, she was not going to London to emigrate, but out of curiosity and to see Lorna. Her education had been influenced by the British system; she had read British books, watched British films, and Ronald had told her she must go to participate in the British cultural and sexual revolution. She had grown up with dreams of liberation from British colonial rule, but that struggle had divided the country and caused chaos from which people were fleeing to find their own personal freedom.

She had grown up on a sugar estate run by a British company, Bookers. They had not run it fairly. Once, Cheddi Jagan had held a meeting in Canefield and she had listened to him describing how Bookers exploited the workers and the country; he gave facts and figures that opened her eyes to the injustice on the sugar estates; it made her feel angry towards the British, a feeling that Burnham and his political culture exploited. At the university there was a new hostility to the British influence in education; they wanted to scrap a syllabus that was dominated by English literature and introduce West Indian writing. Now, according to Ronald, British culture was being liberated by the country's rebellious youth; she was curious to see for herself what it was really like.

★

On the day Joan flew to London there was nothing like the excitement that had surrounded Lorna's departure. She had gone to Canefield to tell Mary and Frederick about her plans, give them her financial contribution and tell them about the bank account. Mary seemed worried that she might not return, but Joan reassured her that this was just a holiday. Mary seemed to have got used to her working in Georgetown, but could Mary still be harbouring ideas about her taking charge of the shop? Joan wondered whether her mother was still clinging to the idea that Lorna would one day return from England and fulfil her dreams of success, though as the years passed, she had ceased to speak of Lorna in this way. Maybe Mary could see from the photos that Lorna sent that she was no longer the child to whom she had attached her dreams; Lorna was now an adult, looking more and more like an English woman.

On the plane, Joan thought about how Lorna had left for England when she was only eighteen years old. She was in her twenties now and her studies were almost over. Was she thinking about returning home? Lorna had continued to write and tell her about the life she was living, but she said nothing about returning.

In the photos she sent, Lorna looked conventional in an English kind of way, but when Joan saw her at the airport with her boyfriend, Tony Wilson, she was shocked to see that Lorna looked like a hippie, with her hair very long and unkempt, dressed in a long, flowing velvet blouse with flared sleeves, matching flared trousers and a wide-brimmed, floppy, black velvet hat. She was jumping up and down with excitement.

From the start, Joan did not feel comfortable with Tony. His manner was arrogant; he seemed to dominate Lorna and did not allow her to speak for herself. If Lorna said anything, Tony would interrupt and interpret what she said.

They owned a small, second-hand car, which they were very proud of. Tony said they had worked hard to save up to buy it; it had taken them to Scotland and Wales. Joan thought the car was smelly and dirty. There were cigarette stubs and empty beer cans all over the floor, but this evidently did not bother Lorna and Tony.

They drove her to Chalk Farm, to the terraced house that they shared with three other students. Tony called it "the commune". Joan was shocked to see that Lorna was sharing a bedroom with him. The others were Jonathan Green – described by Tony as "the Jewish bloke", Tony's younger brother, Stephen, and a white South African girl, Megan. The house needed tidying and cleaning, especially the kitchen where the sink was piled high with dirty dishes. The bathroom was also very dirty, with wet towels and clothing strewn on the floor.

Lorna apologised for the state of the house. It was difficult to get everyone to clean up.

Tony said, "We have to call a meeting, and set up a new cleaning rota. People are ignoring the last one we agreed."

One by one, the flatmates arrived. Joan felt uncomfortable as the focus of attention.

Steve, Tony's brother, was the complete opposite of him; he was charming and friendly, and shook her hand enthusiastically. He sat next to her at the dining table and engaged her in conversation, asking whether she had a good trip, and how her parents were. When Jonathan Green arrived, he also greeted her politely, as did Megan.

When they were all together, Megan asked, "What's for dinner?"

"We've got a can of baked beans in the larder, and some bacon and eggs in the fridge," Tony offered.

Steve blushed. "We've got a guest who's just come halfway round the world to visit us. We can't give her bacon, eggs and beans on her first night!"

"Why not?" Tony countered. "Nothing wrong with bacon and eggs! It's all we've got."

Joan said, "I like bacon and eggs. That's fine."

Jonathan Green put his hand in his pocket and placed a couple of notes and coins on the table. "I think we should take our guest out to dinner on her first night in England."

Tony shook his head and grimaced. "Can't afford it. Haven't even got a quid to my name."

Megan said she, too, was broke.

Joan opened her purse and placed ten pounds on the table. Tony glimpsed the wad of notes in her purse and exclaimed, "My god, you're loaded!"

"We can get fish and chips," Lorna suggested.

Joan said she would like that and would buy it for them all.

Tony whooped with delight, took her money, stuffed it in his pocket and got up to leave. "I'll go and get us fish and chips. And a bottle of wine to wash it down. There's enough here."

"That's really nice of you, Joan," Steve said. "Very kind of you to feed us starving students."

When Tony returned with the meal, they huddled round the table and ate it straight from the newspapers it was wrapped in.

"We should offer you a plate," Steve apologised, "but we haven't got any clean ones."

Tony gave him a cutting look. "We never have clean plates because no one washes up. We have a rota, but no one sticks to it."

Jonathan went to the sink and began to wash up. Joan went to help him, but he told her that she should not be doing this. "It's bad enough you bought us dinner on your first night! From now, I am going to feed you."

Tony guffawed, called him a "bloody toff" for showing off, and told Joan that Jonathan had gone to a public school; he listened to classical music and went to concerts and opera. "He's not working class like us."

Jonathan protested, "My family came here from Poland with nothing, and had to start from scratch. They worked hard to survive. My father was a tailor and shoemaker in the East End. He'd been a classical musician, and conductor with his own orchestra before he had to flee because they were Jews. In London, he made a living as a shoe salesman and managed to buy a maisonette in Hampstead after he married. He was able to send me to a public school, but that doesn't make him middle class. He's a cockney Jew. Don't call me a toff. I'm a communist, I believe in communism. I joined the communist party."

A fierce argument followed between Tony and Jonathan about whose politics was more left-wing. Tony was a member of the International Socialists who, he claimed, supported the real rank and file workers, whilst Jonathan's Stalinists only worked with the bureaucrats in the trade union movement.

Steve coughed self-consciously and declared that he and Tony were not actually really working-class; both their parents could be described as lower middle-class; his mother was a primary school teacher, his father a railway engineer. He was studying sociology, and he thought he knew enough to say that most people in the UK, including his parents, had middle-class aspirations; they all wanted a good standard of living, to own their own homes, and for their children to have a university education. He thought that their arguments about class and who was more working class was spurious; England was becoming classless.

Tony told him not to be so wet. "You and your socio-logical analysis! Sociology is for people with no politics!"

Joan found herself disliking Tony; he suppressed any-one who expressed their own opinion, especially if it differed from his.

"Anyway, let's stop talking about ourselves," Jonathan said. "Tell us about Guyana, Joan. How is the great Cheddi Jagan? I became a great supporter of his when I read how he stood up to the British government and declared himself a communist. That made him a hero in my eyes. When I met Lorna, and heard she came from Guyana, I was pleased to meet someone from that great man's country. I'd hoped Lorna would take me to Guyana. She's always been very popular with us. When she came, everyone wanted to know her, especially my good friend Tony, and as you can see, he got the girl from Guyana."

Joan said, her confidence boosted by the unaccustomed wine, "I'm amazed that you all think Guyana's politics are so wonderful. They've destroyed the country. People in Jagan's party fought over power, and racialised politics, and the country has become racially divided, perhaps perma-nently. It's been a disaster. It started an exodus from the country, people fleeing to live in North America, because the old infrastructure of the country collapsed. A lot of damage was done; the country is in ruins. Communism accomplished nothing in Guyana."

They looked astonished.

She said, "From a distance you can idealise Guyana, but you don't know the reality."

Jonathan asked if she had ever supported Jagan.

She replied, "Yes, I supported him because, like me, he came from a sugar estate. He grew up poor, he saw the poverty and exploitation of the sugar workers. He saw them as the oppressed working people of Guyana, and he wanted to liberate them; this is why he became a communist and politician. I heard his speeches when he came to our sugar estate, and I was impressed by his knowledge of the facts and figures of how Bookers were exploiting people, so yes, I supported and admired him, but I think he failed to unite the country behind him. People in the towns were afraid of him, and he never reached out to them. This failure to unite the country was terrible; it divided and destroyed us, so I would not treat him like a hero or a God. He had his strengths but also weaknesses. He wanted to save the country from British colonialism but it has led to American colonialism now. Forbes Burnham was put in power by the American government; it has all led to a worse colonialism, it has been a disaster for us."

Joan concluded that they were so idealistic, they could not accept reality. To them, politics was just a fad, like the pop music they listened to, that changed every day, giving them new singers and new songs to idealise. Their lives were so comfortable, so full of pleasure, they did not understand what it was like to live in an underdeveloped, third-world country that was easily destabilised. They read politics like a comic book; their heroes were Che Guevara, Mao Tse Tung and Ho Chi Minh. Politics was like a form of entertainment to them.

In the first week that she stayed with them, she saw more of how sheltered their lives were. Their university education was free, and on top of that, they received what they called "a grant" from the government – money to help them live; they also received help to pay their rent. When she told them that she was a part-time university student in Guyana, and was working to support herself and pay her fees, they were shocked to hear that this could be so in Cheddi Jagan's country. They found it unthinkable that anyone should have to pay their own university fees, and did not receive money from their government to help them through university.

"You don't know how well-off you all are," she told them. "You idealise communism, but you could not live in a third world or communist country. I wish I had grown up like you, with a free education. You've no idea what a very good life you have. I'm shocked to come here and find that the British have provided so well for their own people, but in their colonies, they allowed people to live in poverty and deprivation. I'm shocked by the difference. My parents struggle for every penny they have; Lorna and I grew up very poor. I did not go to high school because my parents could not afford the school fees. I had to educate myself privately. You don't know how lucky you are."

Lorna told Joan that she and Tony planned to get married when they completed their degrees, and they took her to meet his parents in Acton. Tony said he did not think his parents would get to meet Lorna's, since they had never travelled abroad, were afraid to and couldn't afford it, so it would be good for them to meet at least one member of Lorna's family.

Tony claimed so strongly to be working class that despite what Steve had admitted, Joan was still surprised to see the large semi-detached house in which his parents lived; it seemed to her that they were housed very comfortably, and must be well off, and therefore, middle class. She told Tony this, and he protested, saying that his parents did not own the house; it was council property for which they paid rent. Only people who owned their houses could be called middle class.

Joan made no reply; she had nothing to compare Tony's family to. When she watched television with Lorna and her flatmates, she listened to their comments about whether it was a middle-class or working-class person on the screen, and she began to deduce that what seemed important to them was that the middle class spoke in one way – what Tony called "posh" – and the working class in another.

Tony's parents were watching television when they arrived. They were just sitting down to watch the start of the Grand National horse race, evidently some big traditional event. His mother invited Joan to sit next to her, and offered her a drink of orange squash. When the Queen appeared on the screen, and they played the national anthem, Tony's parents stood to attention, and Mrs. Wilson touched Joan's arm to hint that she should stand too. In the new republic of Guyana, the British monarch was no longer owed respect, so Joan did not stand up, nor did Tony and Lorna.

Tony told his parents that these days nobody stood to attention for the Queen, and they should stop doing it; the British empire no longer existed; all the former British colonies were now independent; like Guyana, where they had kicked out the British.

"Don't be so rude," his father chided him. "The British empire was a great thing. It made us a great nation. It made this country what it is today. It civilised the colonies."

"Rubbish!" Tony declared.

His mother said, "Don't argue with your father, dear."

"I can argue with whom I like," Tony insisted. "Don't treat me like a child."

His mother said to Joan, "When he comes to see us, he just wants to fight. He criticises us all the time, says he does not like how we brought him up. He says he is a communist now, calls us petty bourgeoise. He says he wishes he'd been born working class, but he's ashamed of us; we are not good enough for him; now that he's getting a university education, he's become a political snob."

She shook her head ruefully.

"You're talking crap," Tony told her. "You sent me to university to get a degree and join the middle class, to get a mortgage, buy a house and give you grandchildren, but I'm not going to do it, never!" And all afternoon, he was ill-mannered and spoke to them with contempt.

"Where's the tea?" he demanded, when he was hungry.

His parents laid the table with bread and butter, ham, cheese, tomatoes, and a sponge cake. Joan could see that it was a simple, modest tea. They were clearly not that well-off, and clearly hurt by Tony's ill-mannered behaviour, but he seemed proud of himself, not ashamed of how badly he treated his parents.

When they returned to the "commune", Steve asked how their visit to his parents had gone. Lorna shrugged and said, "The usual arguments."

Tony said, "They were watching the bloody Grand National; we had to sit and watch it with them."

"Bloody parents," Megan said. "I can't stand mine either. They do nothing but watch television. Bloody middle-class blood suckers."

They did not want to settle down; they wanted to continue to live like rebels. Joan saw how university life had liberated them from their families, had given them the money and the freedom to do as they liked. They spent their days listening to pop music, smoking cannabis and enjoying their sexual freedom. They studied for their degrees, but life was also like a holiday; they had enough money to travel and see the world. Hitchhiking was popular with them. Lorna said that before they bought their car, she and Tony used to hitchhike around England.

Joan was surprised how easily Lorna fitted into this student life. It was nothing like the life their mother had dreamed for her. Mary had imagined that England would

133

prepare Lorna for the life of a successful, middle-class person in Guyana, but England had done the opposite: it had turned her into a hippie who rejected the middle-class life. It seemed to Joan that if Lorna did marry Tony, he would never permit her to live the life of a middle-class person, neither in England nor Guyana.

Jonathan Green was not ashamed of being middle-class. He took Joan to see *La Bohème*, to Indian restaurants and to Hampstead where he had grown up and gone to public school. She enjoyed the opera, though it was new and strange to her, their walks on Hampstead Heath and their conversations, especially when they discovered the similarities between their families. He made her think about her family history in new way.

One day, when he asked her if she had ever visited China, she told him about Clarice Chung.

"My father's mother was supposed to have come from China with her family, but I never met any of them, I only heard stories about them, incredible stories about how they became wealthy and prominent in Georgetown. These stories were told to me like legends, to impress on me what a great Chinese legacy I have, and must continue to possess. My mother's mother, Susan Leo, was also Chinese, but born in Guyana, and her daughters compared her unfavourably with my other grandmother because she was very poor and struggled through a difficult life; she was not seen as leaving any great legacy like Clarice Chung. I found this difficult because I knew Susan Leo well when I was a child and loved and admired her. Susan did not idealise herself as a Chinese person like Clarice; in fact, she adopted an Indian identity and loved Indian men, though her daughters hated her doing this. I grew up feeling caught between these two Chinese grandmothers. To me, the Chinese legacy is a very difficult one."

It was the first time she had ever shared this feeling with anyone.

He laughed and said, "That is exactly like my Jewish legacy. As I've mentioned, my father was a Polish Jew; his family fled Nazi persecution and settled in the East End. They were a large family of brothers and sisters and I found their approach to being Jewish extremely confusing. It sounds like my Polish grandmother was just like your Chinese grandmother. I think she made up stories to help us deal with being Jewish in England and fit in. She approached being Jewish in a way that would encourage us to become respectable. She divided us up into two kind of Jews – Ashkenazi and Sephardic. She said that those of us who were dark, like me, were Sephardic, and these were the kind of Jews who would be failures, while the ones who were fair and blonde, like my brother, would be clever and successful. The dark ones, of course, were easily identified as Jews and suffered discrimination; the ones who were fair passed as English and would do better. Anyway, the family believed in this myth, and it made us strive to fit in and become English. My Jewish family is riddled with these complexes. They strove to become English and middle class; they tried to avoid being like any of the stereotypes they thought the British had of Jewish immigrants. It sounds to me like the same happened to your Chinese ancestors. They fled China, looking for a better life in British Guiana. They had to create a new identity for themselves, and they invented one, like my family. We are quite similar, we have in common an immigrant background, and a struggle to find a new identity in a new country."

Joan was not certain if his interpretation of their similarity was wholly accurate, but he seemed to be genuine in offering his friendship, and she liked the fact that he was more generous towards his family than the other students, though, like them, he professed to be a revolutionary. He admired Chinese communism and Mao, and told her that she should visit China. She told him that she would like to go to China, but to look into the origin of her ancestors. He said that if she liked, he would go with her. At school and in the streets he had suffered racial attacks when he wore his *kippah* and he had been deeply affected by stories about the holocaust; he wanted to end injustice and this is why he believed in communism, as a leveller of society; he believed in making people equal because it would end racism. He gave her a copy of Mao's little red book, as if he were giving China back to her. Despite what Joan had said, he still admired Cheddi Jagan for challenging the British and U.S governments with his communism. He referred to Janet Jagan by her Jewish name, Janet Rosenberg, said he admired her for her relationship with Cheddi Jagan, a marriage based on communist principles. He was sorry that Jagan's communist revolution had failed, but he still wanted to visit Guyana. Joan saw him as a dreamer, full of romantic political ideas, but she liked him for his generosity of spirit, and was happy in his company. In his room, he played her his favourite classical music, and prepared Jewish food for her, bought at the local Polish delicatessens.

Lorna and Tony noticed their growing closeness and tried to turn Joan against Jonathan, but she ignored them; she thought they were prejudiced against him because he was middle-class and Jewish.

★

The day before Joan was due to fly home there was a telephone call from Guyana. It was a message from her father, asking her to come home at once, because her mother was very ill. Steve had answered the phone and relayed the message to them. She and Lorna looked at each other in shock and stood rooted to the ground. It must be serious for their father to instruct Joan to return home "at once".

Joan exclaimed, "Oh God!" and Lorna asked Steve, "They didn't say if I must go home too?" Steve shook his head, and said, "Only Joan. He said it is Joan who must come home, at once. He didn't mention you. Sorry."

DEATHS

All the flight back to Guyana, Joan felt sick with foreboding, and when she arrived at Annie Chung's house, Annie lost no time in telling her, even before she set down her suitcase, "Your mother is dying in New Amsterdam hospital; go home at once, your father say. She is really sick."

She went home to find Frederick in pieces, his eyes puffy from lack of sleep, unshaven and unkempt from not looking after himself. Mary was not yet dead but he was already grieving for her. Joan found herself more worried about him than her mother, for she had never seen him so vulnerable and distraught and this pained her, more even than it pained her when she entered the hospital and saw Mary looking so wasted and diminished. She was more afraid of losing her father then she was of losing her mother, and she suspected that Mary knew this. This guilty secret came between them now when Mary needed her more than ever, to shield her from the pain of death.

Instead of telling her this, Mary complained, "You take so long to come home." So her mother needed her, Joan thought, yet it was only a need for Lorna she had ever displayed to the world – Lorna who was back in England nursing her hurt that her mother did not want her there when she was dying.

Joan nursed Mary dutifully. She combed her hair, she bathed and dressed her with the tenderness of a mother, a tenderness that Mary had never known from her own

138

mother. She fed her like an infant, sat with her until she fell asleep and sometimes stayed with her until she woke again. For the first time ever there was a closeness and a sense of love between them. But because Mary said nothing about Lorna, Joan suspected she was never out of Mary's mind. Did she wish it was Lorna, not Joan, who was looking after her? That was what she had long been waiting for, for Lorna to return from England to take care of her. But none of this was said.

One day, though, Mary asked Joan about Lorna. "I know you see Lorna in England. How she doing?"

"She is fine, studying hard to pass her exams this year."

"I worried about she. I don't like how she look in the photos she send. She look sickly, like she don't eat good, and I see a man with her in the photos. She got a man now?"

"Lorna eating good, Lorna is doing good. She want to come and see you. She don't have no man, she too busy studying."

"I don't want her to come and see me like this. You musn't send for her. Let her study and do her exam. Don't let her come and see her mother so sick. You must promise me. Let her remember me looking nice."

Joan promised not to send for Lorna and once she got this assurance, Mary breathed her last breath.

Joan had to return to Canefield to tell Frederick and her brothers that Mary was dead. Frederick burst into tears, and wailed for Mary, declaring he wanted to die now, he could not live without her. Joan wept too, she wept for him and his sense of abandonment. She did not feel abandoned by her mother, she felt free and was appalled with herself for not feeling any grief, only emotional exhaustion, as if Mary had exhausted her all her life and at last she was free from her. Frederick told her to go to the post office and send a telegram to Lorna, to let her know that her mother had died. At the post office, Joan decided to send the telegram with just the wording, "Come home at once."

Lorna returned just before they closed Mary's coffin, in time to see her wearing her mask of death, and not the look of pleasure and satisfaction Lorna had always drawn from her. When she was in England, Lorna had given Joan no sign that she thought about her place in her mother's dreams, but here, in front of the coffin, it was different. Joan suspected that Lorna felt some guilt – for rejecting the burden of expectation – when she said she had always looked forward to the day she would fulfil her mother's dreams, when she returned from England with her degree. Why had they not told her before? Now she had returned too late, to find Mary dead and the dream ended. She took her confused feelings out on Joan. It was made worse by people continually telling her that Joan had done so well and earned so much money that she had been supporting her parents. Even though nobody said it, Joan was sure Lorna suspected that they all thought how ironic it was, such a twist of fate, that the daughter in whom Mary had placed all her hopes had not fulfilled them, but rather, it was the daughter whom she had not placed on a pedestal who, by the chance created by these changing times, had achieved them. Lorna declared it broke her heart not to fulfil her mother's hopes of salvation.

Joan wondered about her feelings, but convinced herself that the situation did not give her any satisfaction, for she had always seen Lorna's privilege as her curse.

After they buried Mary, Frederick grieved so much it broke his heart, literally, and he had several small heart attacks. Joan took extended compassionate leave and returned home to help him run the shop. She obtained a loan from the bank and invested it in repairing and refurbishing the shop and although the sugar estate was failing, the shop began to prosper. This gave Frederick hope and seemed to bring him back to life for a time, and he hoped that Joan would return home for good, take Mary's place and run the shop with him.

In fact, it was Lorna who came to live with him. She returned from England without completing her degree. She and Tony wanted to live like hippies in Guyana; they did not want to get married and settle down to live a conventional middle-class life; they would settle in Canefield and run the shop and live a subsistence lifestyle like the sugar estate workers – a true working-class life, Tony said. So when they took up residence in the shop, Joan returned to Georgetown to resume her job and live with Annie Chung.

It was not long, though, before she was called back to Canefield because Frederick suffered another heart attack and died. She returned to bury him in St. Peter's graveyard. Annie Chung returned with her; she wanted to bury Clarice Chung's son next to his mother, and they did this to please her.

There was the question of what to do with Clarice's ancestral heirlooms from China – the scroll picture of Emperor Chengzong, the silver coins and purse of seeds of the plum tree and soya beans that their Chinese ancestors brought from China in 1879, which Frederick had pre-served. Annie wanted the heirlooms returned to China. She told Joan, "You got to go to China, and take back these things to where our ancestors come from, take back these things where they belong."

Joan shocked Annie by telling her she had absolutely no desire to go to China. Annie protested that the Chinese were the best race in Guyana, and her Chung ancestors were proof of this. She should be proud that her grandmother Clarice Chung came from China, she was lucky to have such an ancestry.

"I don't have only one Chinese grandmother," Joan said. "My mother's mother, Susan Leo, was Chinese too."

"Yes, I know about her," Annie retorted. "I hear she used to dress like a coolie and had children for a coolie man who treat her bad; she was so poor, she used to beg in George-town, sit down by Bookers with all her pickney and beg, and she give away her children to other people to mind. Your other grandmother, Clarice Chung, was better. When her family come here from China, they punish and suffer, but they raise themselves up. One by one, those Chung brothers manage to escape from that Soesdyke estate and open shops in Georgetown. The eldest one, Arnold Chung, send his sons to study in England, one of them became Chief Justice, the other one turned into the richest man in the country. They were great people, you should be proud you have their Chinese blood!"

"I am more proud of Susan Leo," Joan replied. "She suffered but she was a great woman too! I knew her and I love her more! I did not know Clarice Chung. My aunties told me she was a bad, cruel woman; she tormented them, especially my mother."

Annie shook her head and refused to hear any more. She said, "You can't compare Clarice Chung and Susan Leo. Clarice Chung work hard. She make the Chinee cake, and it sell so much all over the country it make her father-in-law rich. She buy a sewing machine, and sew clothes to sell in that shop, and make money for them. That woman could work, but the big fire burn down their shop in 1913, and she and John had to go back to Soesdyke estate and open a small shop and look after the whole family. When her husband die, Clarice was looking after his parents, too, and her three children, and when his parents want to go to

Berbice, Clarice took all her family to Canefield and start that shop from scratch. She was a great woman; you wouldn't be here if it wasn't for her! She is the grandmother you should be proud of! Not Susan Leo!"

This was a side of Clarice that Joan had not much thought about. She had never known Clarice, only her legend, the myths about her. Her father had told her about the Chungs coming on the last ship from China and how Clarice used to tell him that this was what made them so wealthy and successful, unlike the Hakka Chinese who had come before and lost all their Chineseness – like Susan Leo.

Joan had always thought of Clarice Chung as a manipulative bully, and had rejected her legacy, though when she had met Jonathan Green in London, and he compared Clarice to his Polish Jewish grandmother, and said that Clarice, like his grandmother, was only an immigrant who was struggling to adjust to a new country, it had softened her attitude. What Annie was telling her now about Clarice's struggle to raise her family fitted the image that Jonathan had offered. But in criticising Susan Leo, Annie Chung was also reviving Joan's old feelings of antagonism; she would not abandon her affection for Susan.

It was clear to Joan that since Frederick's death and her own rapid aging, Annie Chung saw herself as the last remaining Chung in the country. In her loneliness she would talk about her wealthy Chinese ancestors because it was the only thing that lifted her spirits. All her relatives had left the country; it was no longer a safe place for them; Burnham did not want them; it was now a country only for black people who wanted to be African; they were changing their names into African ones and wearing dashikis; they no longer wanted to live with the other races.

Annie paced up and down her house muttering these things angrily, smoking like a chimney. She had only her decreasing circle of Chinese women friends, like her no longer well-to-do-women who lived alone in large, empty houses. Now when they met to play mahjong, they had to pretend they had enough money to afford the stakes.

Joan would return from work to find these women huddled over the mahjong table where they argued and fought over their small winnings. They all smoked heavily and they stopped only to drink wine and eat Chinese roast duck and rice smothered in soya sauce. This was all that was left of the Chinese in Guyana, Joan reflected – lonely old women waiting to die, and smoking, drinking and eating themselves to death, gambling away their diminished fortunes.

Annie smoked so excessively that Joan was not surprised when she was diagnosed with lung cancer, taken into St. Joseph's Mercy hospital and died there. Joan was only a very distant relative of Annie's who had lived in her house at the end of her days, but in her will Annie left Joan the house in Camp Street on condition that she sell it and use the money to go to China and find their ancestors. She also left her the Chinese heirlooms that Clarice Chung had brought from China with instructions that they be returned to their descendants in China.

Meantime, Lorna and Tony grew tired of living in Canefield and struggling with the failing shop. They returned to England; Joan's brothers, Andrew and Philip, emigrated to Canada. There was no one left in Canefield, so they sold the shop and buildings.

Annie's house was the house her mother had wanted to live in, but Joan did not want to live in it, so she sold it, and decided that she would do as Annie asked; she would go to China and return the heirlooms, but first she would visit Lorna and Tony in England and see if she could find a way to live there, and escape the country like everyone else.

BACK TO CHINA

I have not told half of what I saw.
— Marco Polo

It was not until 2000 that Joan travelled to Hong Kong with her ancestral artefacts, to find her ancestors, after almost forty years of living in London. During the long flight, she found herself looking back, not forward. But it was not Annie Chung or her father that she thought about, the ones with a direct line to her Chung ancestors. She had never seen herself as a Chung, but a Wong, the child of her mother, Mary Leo, and father, Frederick Wong, neither of whom had ever spoken a word of Chinese and had a troubled relationship with their Chinese heritage. Mary had never thought of herself as real Chinese because she was only half Chinese, and according to the Chungs, the Chinese side of her was invalidated by her Indian half.

She thought of her maternal grandmother, Susan Leo, pure Chinese, who had found solace in love with Indian men, and in Indian culture. She remembered her in her sari, the bindi dot on her forehead, wearing a nose ring and ankle bracelets, how she used to say that she only looked Chinese, but her soul was Indian – if you could see her soul, and in case you couldn't, she dressed like an Indian to help you out. People looked at her and called her "Chinee" but she pretended not to hear them. For her, being Chinese was a curse, bad luck. She wanted nothing to do with

Chinese culture or the people. There were some Chinese people who had helped her, but they were rare; most had disowned her because they thought she was a disgrace to their race, and because she was so poor. Chinese people were not supposed to be poor, they were supposed to be better than everyone else, and so, when they saw her with her small children, destitute on the streets of Georgetown, they looked away. She had lost China and never wished to find it again in any shape or form.

As Joan flew towards Hong Kong, the memory of Susan Leo made her weep.

She thought about how her aunties called Clarice a *real* Chinese woman, as if this was some mythological creature, and it was true that in Guyana, *real* Chinese people were rare. Joan could recall very few *real* Chinese people in her life. There was Willy Chow, the man her cousin, Dolly, had married. People liked to mimic his accent and laugh at him, with his funny, flatfooted walk – and he had exaggerated these features to entertain people. She had heard the story of how the Chows had brought a couple of young Hong Kong men with them; how they had gone into the forest to catch tapirs and turtles, to kill and cook them. Other than this, and the stories about Clarice Chung, China was to her entirely unknown. Clarice, if the stories were true, seemed a cross between a Chinese Queen Victoria and a female Mao Tse-Tung, someone who imposed her authority on you whether you liked it or not. The thought of Mao Tse-Tung made her smile because she remembered that the first present Jonathan Green had given her when she met him in London in 1968 was the Little Red Book. She recalled how she had talked to him about her Chinese grandmothers, and of being torn between the two. She had told him she was Chinese only in appearance, not in any other way; she spoke no Chinese, she had never been to

China and had no real desire to do so. Perhaps he had given her the Little Red Book as a way of giving her a little bit of China. He had told her that her absence of feeling Chinese was like his absence of feeling Jewish; it made them similar. It shocked her to hear him say that he had no desire to be Jewish because it had never occurred to her that she did not want to be Chinese. She asked him where he got that idea from, and he told her to read *Goodbye Columbus* by Phillip Roth – the second book he gave her. He said it explained the difficulties of being a fourth generation immigrant, which they both were; it explained the difficulties in both their lives.

From the plane, she caught her first glimpse of the fantastic, modern skyline of Hong Kong; a vista that would have pleased Clarice Chung had she been alive to see it – proof of the supremacy of the Chinese in which she believed so ardently. But this was not the Hong Kong the Chungs had left in 1879; this was not the old Hong Kong she had come to look for; this was a modern city built as a copy of New York and the new skyscrapers of the financial heart of London. In Hong Kong, the MTR train slid along with the smoothness of the new Jubilee line in the London underground. Only the Chinese faces and their Chinese speech told her she was in China, nothing else.

She was staying at the university hotel so she could meet a historian who might help her to trace the roots of the Chung family. It was a simpler building, more like she expected a Chinese building to be, with the emphasis on breadth, not height, with the walls like a platform for the sweeping, gabled roof to float over the base. It felt like a refuge from the dominance of glass and steel skyscrapers. There were garden courtyards within the hotel where blossom from the mei trees floated down into the small fountains.

It was a relief to unpack her suitcase, retreat to a garden seat and enjoy the sweet scent of the blossoms and coolness of the fountains. It was these mei tree blossoms that had symbolised China for Clarice Chung's mother, that symbolised her loss and longing. As Joan sat there, these same blossoms fell gently on her, so many she had to brush them away.

The next day, she met her contact at the university, who sent her to see an American historian who, she was certain, knew about the Chungs and the ship on which they sailed to British Guiana; he had researched the missionary group to which they belonged.

She had come to Hong Kong to find the passenger list of *The Admiral*, because it had gone missing from the archives in Guyana. Annie Chung was convinced that the list had been deliberately destroyed by the Burnham government because they were trying to erase the Chinese from Guyana's memory. First they had driven them away by overtaxing them, then they erased their history.

The American historian was very old and frail. As soon as Joan entered his high-rise flat, he told her that he had lived in Hong Kong too long; the people had no manners, especially if you had no money, you were white, old and ill and had no family. She detected in his complaint a hint that he wanted her to pay for his help. It was easy to see that Hong Kong was a place where the exchange of money and services defined people's relationships. In central Hong Kong, the skyscrapers squeezed ordinary people like insects into narrow alleys and streets where they frantically sold and bartered their skills and goods. The historian was an academic who felt superior to the Chinese, but he was like them in feeling he was just a bare survivor in Hong Kong's inhuman architecture, perched precariously on a rocky island that was too steep to provide a secure footing for human movement. He told her that he rarely left his flat now because he could hardly walk.

She told him she had come to find out about the Chungs who left on *The Admiral* in 1879 for British Guiana.

"Oh, those Chungs!" he exclaimed. "An interesting bunch they were." He said this as if to whet her appetite, while he took his time, eking out the little he knew.

She said, "I would like to know who they were, where they came from. Do you know?"

He mused. "They were a mysterious lot! They were strong Christians, very strong; they were good converts. They did a lot for the church in Hong Kong. They built four churches! They brought all their folks into the church; they were very strong Christians. They took in the priests and taught them Chinese and helped them a great deal. That is why they were chosen to go to British Guiana."

"Where were they from?"

"Guangdong. They were Hakkas, like everyone that went to the colonies."

"I thought they were not Hakkas."

"They told everyone they were from North China, and they were aristocrats, but it wasn't true. They were full of pretensions that family; they did it to get superior treatment, but the priests saw through them."

She showed him the scroll of the yellow emperor that Arnold Chung took to British Guiana, and he burst out laughing, saying it was nonsense; they were mass-produced in the thousands, the kind of so-called scroll that could still be bought cheap in any market in Hong Kong; although it was possibly late nineteenth century, probably later, it was still tourist tat.

Joan found this to be true when she scoured the antique shops and stalls in Hollywood Road to ask them to verify the scroll. There, too, it was treated with derision, dismissed as tourist rubbish. On the market stalls she had also seen wooden money boxes like the one her family claimed Arnold Chung had brought to British Guiana. They were tourist tat too, on sale for very little money. It had all been a lie. The Chungs had not come from northern China; they were not descended from Chinese aristocrats; the artefacts they took to British Guiana were fakes. If Clarice Chung or Annie Chung were alive, it would have dismayed them to hear it. It did not dismay her; it was a relief not to have to carry the burden of a fantastic myth, which, all along, had been a delusional lie.

She took the Star ferry to Lantau island and threw the silver coins, soya and mei seeds into the sea, then took the bus to Po Lin monastery where she threw the scroll of the Yellow Emperor into a furnace of incense. Afterwards, she walked the Wisdom Path of the Heart Sutra, where she met a young monk who was handing out mantras in English, to recite on the path. The mantra she chose was: "Renunciation is not getting rid of the things of this world but accepting that they pass away."

As the plane took off from Hong Kong and soared into the sky, she felt as if her own wings were spread and she was flying away forever from all ideological and ancestral ties, and she promised herself never to relinquish her freedom for such ties. Never.

ABOUT THE AUTHOR

Jan Lowe Shinebourne was born in Berbice, Guyana, and educated at Berbice High School and the University of Guyana. She comes from the same area of Guyana as her near contemporaries, Cyril Dabydeen and Arnold Itwaru. After school she worked as a reporter in Georgetown, and contributed to the literary magazine, *Expression*. She began writing in the mid 1960s and in 1974 she was a prize-winner in the National History and Arts Council Literary Competition. In 1987, she was also awarded the Guyana Prize for Literature, in the Best First Book of Fiction category.

In 1970 she moved to London where she lived for almost 40 years, then moved to Sussex where she lives currently.

She did postgraduate literary studies at the University of London. In addition to her work as an author, she has also worked as an editor for several journals, as a political and cultural activist and as a college and university lecturer. She has done reading tours in North America, Europe, the Caribbean and Asia.

She has previously published three novels with Peepal Tree Press: *Timepiece* (1986), *The Last English Plantation* (1988), *Chinese Women,*(2010) and a collection of short stories, *The Godmother and Other Stories* (2004).

ALSO BY JAN LOWE SHINEBOURNE

Timepiece
ISBN: 9780948833038; pp. 186; pub. 1986, 2012; price: £9.99

Sandra Yansen must leave behind the close ties of family and village when she goes away to take up a job as a reporter in Georgetown. But she feels that leaving Pheasant is a betrayal and is confused about where she stands in the quarrel between her mother Helen, who is pro-town and her father, Ben, who is deeply attached to the country and its values.

She finds the capital riven by racial conflict and the growing subversion of political freedom. Her newspaper has become the mouthpiece of the ruling party and she finds her ability to tell the truth as a reporter increasingly restricted. In the office she has to confront the chauvinism and vulnerability of her male colleagues whilst at the same time finding common cause with them in meeting the ambivalent challenges of Guyana's independence.

Yet, uncomfortable as she frequently is in the city, Sandra knows that she is growing in a way that Pheasant would not allow. But when Sandra is summoned home with the news that Helen is seriously ill, and re-encounters the enduring matriarchy of her mother's friends, Nurse, Miss K., Noor and Zena, she knows once again how much she is losing. It is their values that sustain Sandra in her search for an independence which does not betray Pheasant's communal strengths.

Fred D'Aguiar wrote of *Timepiece* 'recovering a valuable past for posterity and enriching our lives in the process' and Ann Jordan in *Spare Rib* reviewed it as 'not a novel to be taken at face value, for its joy lies in the fact that it works on so many different levels… the subtleties and tensions of life are not far from the surface as the author questions the notions of political as well as individual dependence and independence'. *Timepiece* won the 1987 Guyana prize.

The Last English Plantation

ISBN 9781900715331; pp. 182; pub. 1988, 2002; price: £8.99

'So you want to be a coolie woman?' This accusation thrown at twelve-year-old June Lehall by her mother signifies only one of the crises June faces during the two dramatic weeks this fast-paced novel describes. June has to confront her mixed Indian-Chinese background in a situation of heightened racial tensions, the loss of her former friends when she wins a scholarship to the local high school, the upheaval of the industrial struggle on the sugar estate where she lives, and the arrival of British troops as Guyana explodes into political turmoil.

Merle Collins writes: 'Jan Shinebourne captures the language of movement, mime, silences, glances, with a feeling that comes from being deep within the heart of the Guyanese community. In *The Last English Plantation* her achievement lies in having the voices of the New Dam villagers dominate the politically turbulent period of 1950s Guyana... A wonderful and stimulating voyage into the lives behind the headlines, into the past that continues creating the changing present. The voices of the New Dam villagers never leave you.'

Wilson Harris writes: 'Jan Shinebourne's *The Last English Plantation* is set within a labyrinth of political chaos in British Guiana in the 1950s. But the novel is more subtly as well as obsessively oriented towards the psychological as well as the inner landscape of a colonial age. A gallery of lives depicted in *The Last English Plantation* is drawn from diverse strata of cultural legacies and inheritance. The desolations, the comedy of adversity, the contrasting moods of individual and collective character give a ritual, however incongruous, substance to the fate of a dying Empire.'